The Humptons

By

Amanda M Arnold

To Linda,
Best Wishes
Amanda M Arnold

Published by and available from
The Endless Bookcase Ltd
71 Castle Road, St Albans, Hertfordshire,
England, UK, AL1 5DQ
www.theendlessbookcase.com

Printed Edition
Also available in multiple e-book formats via The Endless
Bookcase website, Amazon, Kobo and Nook.

Printed in the United Kingdom
First Printing, 2017

ISBN: 978-1-912243-17-4

Acknowledgement

Once again a big thank you to Georgina for her unstinting help and support. Also my grateful thanks to Morgana whose expertise has proved invaluable throughout.

About the Author

Amanda grew up in North London and after leaving school and college she spent several years working in the fashion world in London.

Relocating to Norfolk she has enjoyed living near to the coast and her interests include art, photography, entertaining and travelling abroad. These topics often find their way into her fiction. She is also an active member of a local Creative Writing group.

'The Humptons' originally started out as a short story, however as she became more intrigued with the characters' lives it developed into a novel.

Characters

Little Humpton Village

Madge Kenton

Jimmy Griggs

Daisy Biggers

Bert Biggers

Miranda Fowler

Keith Fowler

Pixie Dean

Joe Pickering

Billy Pickering

Sir Jolyon Chudleigh

Lady Phyllis Chudleigh

Busby

Tingaling

Doctor Tang

Drusilla Harris

Fanny (Frances) Jones

Harold Jones

Bernard Danvers MP

Miss Emily Millet

Dawn Keeble

Greater Humpton Village

Phoebe Perkins

Thomas Perkins

Gary (Hairdresser)

Harry Mobbs

Sophia Mobbs (Silver)

Betsy Rowe

Bella Rowe

Wally Rowe

Fred Constable

Joan Balcombe

Howard Balcombe

Rodney Smart (The Grudge)

Diamond Jake Blake

Waddlington Major

Professor William Wolfe

Foxley Grange (tenants)

Charles Edward McCreasey the 3rd

Faye McCreasey

Henri Osman

May Bush

Rollo Barnes

Clarence Sparks

Dee Bee

Alain

Public Houses and Restaurants

The King's Arms, Little Humpton

The Hind, Greater Humpton

The Golden Cockerel Restaurant.

Animals

Bluey. A parrot

Satan. A horse

Picasso. A dog

Boomps and Daisy. Dogs.

The Local Autumn Show

Madge placed the wicker basket containing the washed and perfectly shaped carrots into the boot of her mud spattered car, then stood back to gaze with pride at the pick of her crop.

'Beat that Jimmy Griggs.' she muttered.   Then slamming down the tailgate, she drove to the village hall going over the humpbacked bridge that separated Little Humpton from Greater Humpton. The rivalry between the two villages was intense, and none more so than when the inhabitants took part in the Autumn Show.

Meanwhile Daisy Biggers was carefully unpacking her scrumptious looking cupcakes on to a trestle table that was covered with a white tablecloth. She found a space between Miranda Fowler's rather soggy efforts and Fanny Jones's suspiciously shop-bought looking entry. Whenever the village cricket team's members' wives took their cakes and sandwiches for the cricketer's afternoon tea it was always Fanny's sad looking efforts that were left untouched. Although young and pretty, she was also quite shy and retiring.   Her rejected culinary offerings did nothing for her self-esteem.

'Good morning everyone' Madge breezed, 'What time are we expecting our Judges?'

'They said they will arrive promptly at eleven, and they are old school so never late.'   Keith Fowler, the Chairman of Humpton's Horticultural Society replied.

Daisy Biggers smiled as she put her name card against her plate of cakes, making sure Keith saw where they were on the table and would hopefully direct the Judges to them. Daisy had won Best Cake Rosette for the last two years and was hoping to make it three in a row. Yes, a hat trick would be what she deserved.

Madge propped her name card up on her neatly arranged three carrots, the stipulated number. Glancing at Jimmy's three carrots, she noted that they were definitely of an inferior size and shape. As neighbours, they had battled for years over the 'Best Vegetable' category and this year Madge had spent months weeding out her rows of carrots until she had three perfect specimens. Her carrots stood out among the withered and lumpy beetroots and onions that had seen better days.

There was a scrunch on the gravel outside as Sir Jolyon and Lady Phyllis Chudleigh arrived in their Rolls, driven by Busby their chief steward and man of many parts.

A flustered Keith Fowler rushed forward to welcome them, but in his eagerness tripped and fell forward into the large bosom of Lady Phyllis. He regained his composure after untangling himself from her ladyships cleavage, but managed to get her diamond brooch stuck in what little remained of his hair.

'On behalf of Little Humpton's Autumn Show may I...' Keith began, however, by then a harrumphing Sir Jolyon was already inside the hall followed by a distinctly flushed Lady Phyllis prodding her ebony walking stick into anyone in her path.

Miranda already had her heavily bejewelled hand on Sir Jolyon's arm and was steering him over to the cake table.

'These are the cakes made by the ladies of the village.' she said in her breathless, little girl voice. 'The names are on them.' she continued indicating her own name by the worst looking plate of cakes.'

Keith and Lady Phyllis joined them 'We don't have to eat them, do we?' Lady Phyllis queried quite horrified at the thought.

'Only a small amount' said Keith, smoothing his hair and handing the diamond brooch back to Lady Phyllis, who after giving him a withering look, pinned it back on her ample chest.

Sir Jolyon was already on the other side of the Hall where the vegetables were displayed.

'Not as good as those in my walled kitchen garden.' He remarked.

Madge bristled, saying. 'But you have a gardener we grow them ourselves in our back gardens.'

Lady Phyllis joined them. 'Quite right, you tell him,' she boomed adding 'which are yours, my dear?'

Madge indicated her plate then gasped. The names had been switched and Jimmy Griggs's name was beside her plate.

'Someone is cheating.' She exclaimed and switched the names back.

'You can't do that!' Jimmy shouted.

'I just have.' Madge replied.

'This is too much' said Lady Phyllis and followed Sir Jolyon and Miranda into the refreshment tent just in time to see him pinch Miranda, who squealed and Lady Phyllis said witheringly, 'I saw that Jolyon, I have a headache I think I wish to leave.'

It was a command, and not one to be ignored.

As they made their way to the exit passing Madge, Sir Jolyon held her hand up.

'The winner of the vegetable class' he said. Then looking round spotted a downcast looking Fanny, 'and this lady is the winner of the cakes, well done.'

With that, the Judges climbed into the Rolls and as they were whisked away, Lady Phyllis could be seen giving Sir Jolyon a piece of her mind.

'What a shambles' Jimmy Griggs remarked, staring sadly at his second class carrots.

'That should teach you not to try and cheat,' Madge said, as she picked up her plate of carrots with the winners rosette, then swept out to her car.

'Just accepted strategic manoeuvres, as practiced on the battlefield.' Jimmy shouted after her. He had been in the army before retiring and his life was still run on army lines.

This year not a single member of Greater Humpton Village received even a runner's up mention.

'Quite understandable,' said Thomas Perkins defensibly, he was the Chairman of their Horticultural Society, 'we get more rain on our side of the river than the Little Humpton lot.'

'What tosh,' fumed Jimmy Griggs, 'you will just not admit our members in Little Humpton produce better exhibits.'

'Well my carrots were waterlogged for months' Thomas replied.

'Drainage, my dear chap, drainage.' said Jimmy, 'get your troops ready for next week's Knotted String Battle, we may win that as well.'

Jimmy had been quite "top brass" in the Army and while his carrots were not up to scratch, he shone in the local re-enactment tournaments.

'I am running the show for Little Humpton again,' he said, 'my past military experience will come in very handy, though of course on a much smaller and less bloody scale.'

'The American tenant of Foxley Grange, Charles Edward McCreasey is our man for Greater Humpton this time. I feel I must not hog the limelight.' Thomas replied modestly, as Phoebe his wife joined him, and they left quickly bearing their rather pathetic looking entries.

Miranda threw her soggy cakes in the rubbish bin and ignored Keith's efforts to placate her. It would take a nice piece of jewellery and a long Cruise to put him back in her good books.

A flushed and beaming Fanny packed the shop bought cakes into her carrier bag and pinned her winner's rosette onto the handle.

'Well that was a success,' Chairman, Keith said, 'roll on next year.'

The Knotted String Historical Society

Drusilla Harris threw the last tabard she had been sewing onto the large pile on the floor and stretched her aching legs. 'That's it, my treadle feet have had It.' she said to Fanny Jones, who was knitting grey, hairy string into sleeves for the knights' armour. The sweet and long suffering Fanny, ignoring her red and raw fingers replied. 'Well I think we deserve a decent part in the Battle on Saturday for all this work'.

As she packed up her cotton reels and scissors into her shopping bag, Drusilla gave her a pitying look; Fanny was too sweet for words. 'Don't hold your breath, with those uppity Americans in charge, we will be lucky to get any part other than lying dead in a field. By the way have you noticed how tight Faye is, she never has any money on her when we are in the pub after a battle.'

'Perhaps Americans don't carry money, a bit like Royalty. Faye always says that she does not have her Purse with her'. Fanny said as she put on her coat and turned off the lights.

'By purse she means handbag, and Americans pay the earth for swanky designer handbags. No, I have never seen her buy a drink and yet she is never slow to ask for a fancy cocktail if someone else is buying.' Drusilla was well known for not mincing her words.

The next Saturday the members of The Knotted String Society assembled on the Common below the ruins of Little Humpton's Castle. Madge Kenton had been recruited as Drummer Boy for the defenders' side being the tallest lady in the village and therefore highly visible. Although her dreary drumming did not rouse the troops to greater efforts. There was a shortage of archers and sword-carrying soldiers, so the next size down ladies were given the parts of boy foot soldiers, and told to make lots of noise banging their silver painted, wooden swords on their tin foil covered cardboard shields.

The Little Humpton's village side was led by Jimmy Griggs who though retired and not the youngest member, was the star of the local gym at the Health Club. He always put weight training and body building on his C V as his main hobby when applying for membership of clubs.

The foreign attackers' side from Greater Humpton's village, had Charles Edward McCreasey the third, as their leader. Charles and Faye were renting a large house in Greater Humpton while he researched the history of his ancestors whom he was sure were related to Kings and high ranking nobility.

Charles prided himself on his horsemanship and had borrowed a large piebald horse with a deceptively sweet face and a fierce hatred of humans for the battle. The horse was called Satan and would play nice until it suited him to go berserk. Charles was unaware of Satan's shortcomings, as the owner bore him a grudge and had not relayed this to Charles. However, the watching crowd knew of Satan's reputation and were looking forward to him kicking off.

Sir Jolyon and Lady Phyllis Chudleigh were sitting on fold up camp chairs among the ruins of the Castle. Lady

Phyllis was wearing a green moth-eaten velvet dress that she had found in a dressing up chest in the attic of Frogitt Hall, their rather dilapidated country seat.

As the weather was chilly, she had over it, the long red robe with white ermine trim that had belonged to her father, Lord Frogitt. To look even more grand and worthy of saving, she added the diamond tiara that she had worn when being presented at Court, more years ago than she cared to remember.

By contrast, Sir Jolyon had downplayed his ensemble, opting for his shooting gear of plus fours, tweed jacket and deerstalker hat.

The aim of the attacking side was to capture Sir and Lady Chudleigh, while the defenders would try to stop them. It was a sell-out show with all ages attending.

The proceedings started at precisely two o'clock with a violent drum roll from Madge, who even startled herself and used up so much energy that from then on she just made do with single beats. The attackers surged forward uttering blood curdling cries, with Charles the third on Satan and Faye also on a borrowed horse, resplendent in a 'Maid Marian' type outfit, complete with a flowing scarf headdress.

Drusilla and Fanny, dressed in dreary sacking dresses had been allotted the role of 'Trollops', the least glamorous of the parts given out by Charles. As they passed a group of local schoolboys who were jeering everyone, Billy Pickering asked cheekily, 'What do you do?'

Drusilla struggling over the rough grass hissed, 'You are too young to know about things like that; ask me when you are older'.

There was a stunned silence from the boys as they tried to work that one out.

The noise was deafening, the attackers were moving Jimmy Griggs's men back up the incline towards the ruins, when Satan decided it was time for his party piece. Whinnying loudly, he reared up on his hind legs and took off at lightning speed, Charles the third, clinging desperately to his neck. Maid Marian or Faye, sitting side-saddle on her horse, hadn't a chance as it dutifully followed, and when they reached a small copse of trees, a low branch caught in her flowing head dress and she was pulled unceremoniously off her horse, and left dangling a few feet from the ground.

Charles the third meanwhile, was miles away as Satan was really enjoying his afternoon canter, but when they came to the riverbank Satan came to a dead stop. Charles flew like a bird for what seemed to him like miles and landed in the middle of the murky depths of Humpton Reach. The river was well known for its angling and a couple of weekend anglers were not pleased to have the quiet waters disturbed.

'Oy, Can't you read the sign? It says no swimming here.' one said. While his mate called out. 'Blithering idiot, I had a really big fish on my line and now it's gone, shove off!'

'Terribly sorry' Charles gasped, struggling towards the bank covered in slimy weed.

'Ah,' said the first angler, noting Charles accent. 'American! They have never forgiven us for the War of Independence, always reliving the Boston Tea Party. Sacrilege I say, wasting all that tea, I could do with a cup right now.'

Charles was now trying to climb up the bank but all the water pouring off him made him slide back into the river.

The anglers in the interest of good relations put down their rods and each grabbed one of Charles's hands. Having pulled him out they also tried to catch Satan who was enjoying the chase and was leading them a merry dance.

'Got a lively beast there' one puffed. 'He looks a bit like Jeremy Parkers old horse, Satan that he saves for people who have upset him.'

'That is who lent Satan to me, and yes we did have an argument about politics'. Charles said as he finally grabbed hold of Satan's reins.

The two anglers fell about laughing. 'Well if I were you I wouldn't get up on Satan's back again. You had better just walk him back and hope he behaves himself.'

Charles thanked them, and the two men settled down again to their fishing while Satan and Charles started the long walk back. Charles telling Satan his life story in the hope that it might stop him taking off again. Satan was warming to Charles and also feeling a bit tired so trotted happily along.

When they came to a five bar gate beside a stile on a bridle path, Charles sat down on the stile as he was in no hurry to get back to the battle. Satan, who had pricked up his ears when Charles got to the part about his ancestors fighting Red Indians when their landing party was ambushed, leant against the gate and appeared to listen. Charles was enjoying being able to talk without Faye interrupting him, as she usually did and grew more eloquent by the minute.

Back at the battle, the tide was turning and although the attacking army had reached Sir Jolyon and Lady Phyllis, those two imposing figures had joined in, Lady Phyllis wielding her walking stick and Sir Jolyon his rolled umbrella. It was a fearsome sight especially as Lady Phyllis's tiara, had become dislodged and was tipping to one side. The sun at that moment came out and glinted off it, blinding the attackers. Lacking their leader to urge them on, the bugler sounded the retreat and the routed attackers fled.

'Well done our brave defenders!' Sir Jolyon shouted, after climbing up on what remained of one of the towers. 'Lady Phyllis and I invite you all back to Frogitt Hall for tea.'

The victors and vanquished cheered and trooped along together. Back at the Hall the faithful Busby and his wife called Tingaling, had tea, sandwiches, scones and cakes waiting, and it was all very jolly. Tingaling came from some far-flung country and because some people could not understand her high bell like voice or pronounce her name, she answered to that. Busby, who had worked for Sir and Lady Chudleigh for years, had found Tingaling on a dating site and they were both very happy and pleased, as were their employers at getting a 'buy one get on free' in the employee department.

As Charles had not appeared, Faye joined the others in the 'King's Arms', Little Humpton's only pub, for a drink. After downing her third Cocktail, Faye stood up and announced she really must be on her way.

'Hang on a minute,' Jimmy said, 'It is your turn to buy the next round of drinks.' As expected Faye said she did not have her purse with her.

'Landlord please come and explain to Faye the age old tradition we have in this country of what happens if customers cannot buy their round when it's their turn'.

The Landlord, who had been alerted to Faye's habit of never having any money on her, came out from behind the Bar.

'You will have to come with me to the kitchen and wash up. It's very fortunate for me, as tonight I am shorthanded in the kitchen as my pot boy is on holiday.'

A red-faced Faye stood up and followed him behind the Bar as the others hid their delight.

'That solves that one I think'. Jimmy remarked, just as a mud splattered Charles entered the Bar.

Good Lord, are you okay?' Joe Pickering, Pixie Dean's other half enquired.

'Never better thanks,' Charles replied, 'where is Faye?'

'Washing up'. The assembled mixed bag of troops replied.

'Faye has never washed up in her life, how did that happen?' A bemused Charles said.

'No money on her for her round', several voices chorused.

Charles laughed. 'Let her stew for a bit, she extracts what she can from everyone including me. By the way did we win?'

'It was a good fight but you lost, bad luck.' Jimmy said, making way for Charles to sit down even though there was a lingering smell of Humpton Reach about his person.

'Well Satan and I did become quite good chums on the return journey however, I am sure if I ever got on his back again he would still take off. Anyway, what are you all drinking, my turn to buy a round?'

Faye in the kitchen, up to her elbows in soapy water, wondered what all the cheering was about.

The Undoing of Charles

The main reason for Charles Edward McCreasey's stay in Greater Humpton village had been to research his family history. He lost no time pursuing this after the 'Knotted String Society' battle was over, driving on the following Monday to see the area's expert, who lived in Waddlington Major, the next village along.

Rumours abounded about the goings-on in that neighbourhood, with tales of naked dancing in the graveyard after dark. However, when Charles knocked on the door of Frantley House and a rather whiskery figure in a velvet smoking jacket answered the door, it all seemed quite respectable.

'Come in my dear fellow, I was expecting you. So nice to meet a visitor from the other side of the pond, my name is Professor Wolfe, but you can call me William '

'Thank you William, I am Charles Edward McCreasey the third and I believe you are an expert at tracing one's ancestors if they had ever lived in this area.'

The Professor led the way down numerous dark passages until they came to what appeared to be his study. He seated himself behind a large wooden desk and indicated to Charles to take the chair in front of him.

Charles cleared his throat and taking a folded sheaf of papers out of his pocket handed it over the desk. 'As you can see I have written down what I have been told of my family's history. Charles Edward McCreasey the second was my late father, who lived all his life on his inheritance and never had to work. His father Charles Edward McCreasey invented a machine that revolutionised laying railway tracks and made the family fortune. I have always been told that we are related to Bonnie Prince Charlie and hope you can prove this is the case. In my hometown, our family is held up as an example of all that is good and noble. Our position in the community, due to our connection to Royalty, is the envy of most people.

The Professor stroked his hairy chin. 'When did you say your relative first went to America?' he asked,

'A Charles Edward McCreasey who was born and lived in Waddlington Major village was on the Mayflower list of passengers when it landed in Cape Cod. We always believed he was the son of Bonnie Prince Charlie. His mother was a great beauty and though she never married, she did have a son. My family believe that in spite of her humble origins, the Prince was the baby's father.' Charles replied.

The Professor shook his head. 'Sorry to disillusion you but your dates do not add up. The Mayflower sailed from Plymouth on the 6th September 1620 and Charles Edward Stuart was not born until 31st December 1720, so if your ancestor was on the Mayflower that is not possible.'

Charles looked so downcast William said , 'All is not lost, you said the member of your family that went on the Mayflower came from this village so let us look in the archives, in the church and see if we can find any reference.'

They did indeed find a reference in a very dusty old book, in a room at the back of the church. William perched a pair of spectacles on his nose and after leafing through several pages, he stopped and read out; 'Charles Edward McCreasey, wanted for stealing a sheep, absconded while being apprehended'. Shaking his head he said, 'I am afraid your ancestor was a common criminal who ran away to America long before Bonnie Prince Charlie was born. I would think he was, in fact, a stowaway.'

Charles looked shattered. All those years of telling everyone of his illustrious lineage had just come to a full stop.

'If I were you,' William said kindly 'I would keep quiet and say nothing. What people don't know can't hurt you. Too much information is a bad thing, I will say nothing about this to anyone.'

As Charles was leaving, he shook William's hand. 'Thank you, even if it was not the news I wanted to hear, it was lovely meeting you,' and with that he sped off back to Greater Humpton village. When Faye eagerly asked what had transpired, Charles mumbled that it was all very disappointing and nothing had turned up.

The following week the McCreaseys flew back to Connecticut, cutting short their visit.

'That is a shame.' Jimmy Griggs said, 'Charles promised to give a talk at the next Knotted String Society meeting about his connection to Royalty. Now I will have to ask Professor Wolfe to give a talk on common criminals in the 17th century, we had a few of them, I believe.'

Funnily enough, Professor Wolfe declined to appear citing other pressing engagements.

What a Pantomime

There was much speculation in Greater Humpton village as to who the next tenants of Foxley Grange would be now that the McCreaseys had left early. As a large moving van drove down the main street and turned into Foxley Road, many a curtain twitched, and Pixie Dean did not see the calming island approaching and fell off her ancient bicycle.

It was October and as always happened at that time of year, the two Humpton Amateur Dramatic societies met together in Greater Humpton's village hall to discuss the Christmas show.

'As we did 'Dick Whittington and His Cat' last year, are there any suggestions?' Phoebe Perkins, the Chair of Greater Humpton's band of Thespians enquired.

There was a chorus of the name of every Pantomime ever performed.

'Rubbish,' shouted the members of Little Humpton's more famous society, 'we should write and perform an original work.' They did this delaying tactic every year knowing no one in Greater Humpton had a clue about writing anything. The meeting broke up in disarray but with the agreement to meet the following week, with hopefully some suggestions.

'Guess who has moved into the vacant house in Foxley Road?' a breathlessly excited Phoebe said when she went to have her usual wash and blow dry at Gary's Unisex Hair Salon, 'only the famous TV producer, May Bush.' Thomas Perkins, Phoebe's husband ran the local estate agents which meant they were first to know who came and went in the two Humpton communities '

'Ooh, I read in one of the gossip magazines that May has left her husband for Henri Osman, the lovely hunk on her evening soap programme'. Gary was gay, and loved gossip even more than his customers did.

'Well I think I will take the bull by the horns and call on May and see if we can get her interested in Greater Humpton's Christmas show.' Phoebe said, as she emerged from under the towel that Gary was using to remove the surplus water from her shoulder-length, dark hair, 'You never know she might agree and it would shut that Madge Kenton up, always coming it because her dear departed husband wrote ghastly poems that were printed in the parish magazine.'

'Worth a try, Darling,' Gary said, brush and hairdryer at the ready, 'now are we going for the curly or straight look this week?'

'Straight please Gary. Oh, my God is that Madge coming up to the window? Now not a word about May Bush.'

As Madge looked in the window, she saw a rather bedraggled Phoebe and waved a gloved hand. Entering the shop, she gushed. 'Darling, just the person I wanted to see. A little bird has told me that a famous person is taking over the tenancy of Foxley Grange. Any idea as to their identity?'

'Oh hello Madge, no not yet but when I do, you will be the first to know.' Phoebe lied. 'What are you doing in Greater Humpton this morning?'

'Nothing special, must fly, see you.' and with another wave Madge was gone.

Gary busy with his brush, waved the dryer at her departing back.

'Sniffing around trying to find out who is moving into the village,' Phoebe shouted above the noise of the dryer, 'Madge always wants to be first with the news. Well, the minute I have finished here I am knocking on the door of Foxley Grange. Thanks Gary, the hair looks very nice.' With that, Phoebe paid and virtually ran out of the shop.

Foxley Grange was a large detached house at the end of a tree-lined drive. As Phoebe walked speedily up to the dark green painted door, she saw a couple of furtive figures hiding in the bushes.

After ringing the doorbell several times, a handsome young man opened the door a crack and peered out.

'I am from the Perkins Letting Agents.' Phoebe lied; it was that kind of morning. 'Just checking all is in order, can I come in?'

'Of course, May will be down soon, she is upstairs on the phone to the Studio. 'My name is Henri.' He was handsome, charming and of course, she recognised him and his lovely drama school type tones from his roles on the television. I wish we could snaffle him for our Christmas show, Phoebe thought as she followed him into the large kitchen, piled high with packing cases.

'Bit of a mess I'm afraid, but we have both been recording the show, and this is our first free day.' Henri said as May Bush entered. If there was a prize for well-preserved females, May would get it. Her skin was tight over her cheekbones, her eyes large and wrinkle free and her navy American size zero trouser suit fitted perfectly. May obviously had a very good plastic surgeon that she visited regularly. Phoebe suddenly felt every inch the country bumkin.

'I just popped in to see if everything was in order'. Phoebe said by way of explanation while thinking it is now or never, I must broach the question of the local show somehow.

'Fine, no complaints so far thank you' May said, with a sweeping gesture towards the front door, that made Phoebe feel like a pile of leaves in autumn.

Phoebe stood her ground. 'In Greater Humpton we put on a Christmas show each year. This year we are thinking of writing a one-off original show, can I ask you to help us out please? We meet in the village hall at seven thirty on Tuesdays.'

Henri recognising this as a cry for help, smiled and turning to May said, 'We can do that can't we Darling?' May who had been considering telling Phoebe to get lost gave a thin smile saying, 'If you want to help Henri go ahead. Now I must get going. Tell Mr Perkins, so far, all is in order'.

'Thank you so much, you are very kind.' Phoebe gushed as she was shown to the door by a frosty May. In the background, Henri smiled goodbye.

As the front door closed Phoebe could hear twigs snapping and the sound of leaves rustling, going over to investigate, a couple of figures, a few feet apart, stood up.

One was a very flustered Madge removing stray undergrowth from her hair and a young man with a professional looking camera.

'Madge what are you doing in there?' Phoebe said trying not to laugh.

There was a long pause and you could almost hear Madge's brain whirring. 'Err; I thought I saw a limping stray cat come into these bushes, I was going to rescue it'. Even Madge thought this sounded a bit implausible.

The young man said, 'I was trying to get a picture of—' his answer was drowned out by a sudden fit of fake coughing from Phoebe who spluttered that it would be great if Madge would help her down the road so she could get a cup of tea at The Copper Kettle tearooms.

'Of course', Madge said, 'I will join you and we can talk about the Show.'

'So embarrassing,' Phoebe said that evening, as she relayed the events of the morning to Thomas, 'However, I didn't say anything about May Bush moving into Foxley Grange, but it will not be long before everyone finds out.'

'Perhaps not' Thomas was very professional and always withheld client's details.

By the next Tuesday, Phoebe had already had a cosy meeting with Henri at the Grange and they had agreed that the show would be called Crusoe's Holiday Island. It would feature well-known characters from several pantomimes. As he was filming late that Tuesday, Henri did not attend the first meeting but promised to write what he could during breaks on the set.

Madge was pushing for 'Little Bo Peep' as a new show she would undertake, insisting that sheep costumes could be easily made by sticking cotton wool onto old tracksuits. A smiling Phoebe countered that by saying that at the next meeting of the Greater Humpton Am Dram Society she would have the script of a new and original show. Once again, the air was toxic and the meeting broke up after much shouting from the committee up on the stage and the assembled members sitting in front of them on chairs.

Later that week Phoebe whooped with delight when Henri handed her the finished script.

'What a darling you are.' She said as she flicked through the quite thick amount of pages in a proper folder adding, 'Get out of that, Madge Kenton, you and your cotton wool sheep.'

Henri laughed, 'I never knew village life was so competitive. It makes Show Business look tame in comparison.'

'You wait and see how bloody it gets when we start casting.' Phoebe replied, 'By the way which part would you like? As you are the author you get first pick.'

Henri thought for a minute then with his customary devastating smile said. 'I would love to be the Long John Silver character; I have always wanted to play him with a live parrot on my shoulder'.

'Old Harry Mobs has a parrot, we can ask if he will agree to lend him to us for the production.' said Phoebe barely able to hide her excitement. 'I will go round right away and ask him'.

Harry was sitting in his usual armchair by the window of his neat old cottage on the outskirts of the village. Although he lived alone, apart from his parrot called Bluey, Harry was in quite good health. Since his wife had died his granddaughter popped in whenever she could and always cooked him a tasty Sunday lunch.

'Wonderful girl,' he would tell people, 'Pretty and sweet, I got them to name her Sophia after the dark and sultry film star. However, she turned out to be blonde and sunny but an angel to me.'

'Come in'. Harry called when Phoebe knocked on his open door.

'Hello Harry, how are you?' Phoebe said, and then she explained about the Christmas show and the urgent need for a live parrot.

Harry was as cagey an old bird as his parrot. 'Oh I don't know about that,' he said, 'Bluey is very particular about who he likes, he may not want to sit on this fellow's shoulder'

Bluey was actually green, but had first belonged to a colour-blind sailor, this also accounted for his often-ripe language. Hearing his name Bluey opened one eye and let a stream of choice swear words drift round the room.

'Oh dear does he do that often?' Phoebe enquired,

'Only in the mornings.' Harry replied, 'After I give him his drop of rum at lunch time he's quite respectable. The bad language is another thing I blame that sailor for.'

'Can we include Bluey in our cast please Harry? The person he will be co- starring with is that very well-known actor Henri Osman.' Phoebe was pulling out all the stops to get Harry to agree.

'Well if you give my granddaughter Sophia a leading role, then you can have Bluey as well.' Harry said, leaning back in his chair with a satisfied look.

'Silly old git' Bluey muttered, hearing his name again.

'Agreed' a relieved Phoebe said getting up and patting Harry on the shoulder, 'we start rehearsing two weeks from now on a Tuesday. Will you tell Sophia I will be in touch'?

With that Phoebe left, well pleased that it was all falling into place.

By the next Tuesday meeting, word had whirled around about Greater Humpton Am Dram's coup of enlisting Henri Osman as author and star. Madge was livid but hoped for a good part as a face saving ploy.

Phoebe started by saying that she would produce and direct the show and then read out the two parts already allocated. 'Long John Silver would be played by Henri Osman and Cinderella by Sophia Mobs.'

'What about the parrot?' Some wag called out, and a jubilant Phoebe relayed that the part had already been cast.

It was agreed Robinson Crusoe would be played by Bert Biggers and because Jimmy Griggs looked good in minimal clothes, due to his body building and all the time spent in the gym, he would play Man Friday.

As Joe Pickering was well over six foot, he was an obvious choice for the Giant. Pixie Dean, Joe's partner was cast as Dorothy from the Wizard of Oz, as she could sing and dance. Fanny Jones and Drusilla Harris were in charge of designing and making the costumes and they were to be dressers on the night. Billy Pickering would play a dwarf as his parents remarked that he could not be left alone in the house, as he was only eight years old. Billy thought this was super as he could then stay up late.

Fred Constable, Greater Humpton's resident police officer was cast as Aladdin and Betsy Rowe from the Post Office, who was also the evening class Yoga teacher, would be Peter Pan. There was speculation as to whether Betsy would be flying or grounded due to 'Health and Safety'.

A panicking Madge, seeing all the best parts being already allocated demanded to know whom she would be. Phoebe scanning down her cast list said, 'One of the ugly sisters Madge'.

'But they are usually played by men, haven't you a part that is a bit more me?' A seething Madge demanded.

'An ugly sister or a tree is all I have left Madge.' Phoebe said firmly.

'Ok' muttered Madge determined to make this an ugly sister of dynamic, dramatic star quality.

The other ugly sister would be Keith Fowler, while his wife Miranda had been given the part of Jack without the beanstalk, as she looked good in tights.

Phoebe announced that Sir Jolyon and Lady Phyllis Chudleigh had kindly agreed to attend the opening night. Tickets were now available and had been selling fast.

The meeting broke up with an excited buzz, only Madge seemed unhappy as she got into her car and drove back to Little Humpton.

When rehearsals started, it was quite a shambles with the cast reading the script on the first Tuesday night. Everyone agreed that Henri had done a good job with the writing. Sophia had never acted before and found it quite hard, so Henri volunteered to coach her as often as he could. They met in the village hall and then continued afterwards in the Pub as Henri, shouting above the noise in the Bar, taught Sophia how to expand her vocal range. Bluey luckily took to Henri, and was very well behaved, sitting on his shoulder. Harry doubled Bluey's rum allowance and that helped with his bad language problem.

The tickets were a sell-out mainly due to everyone wanting to see Henri in the flesh. Sophia was showing real talent as Cinderella, due to the intense coaching sessions at Foxley Grange when May was at the studio.

On opening night, Sir Jolyon and Lady Phyllis Chudleigh took their seats in the front row of the audience in the village hall. Lady Phyllis was resplendent in a low cut brocade cocktail dress, around her neck were several long river pearl necklaces, also ropes of jet and crystal beads rested on her well-endowed bosom and jangled every time she moved. Her favourite diamond tiara was anchored firmly on her head.

'What is the play, Phyllis old girl?' Sir Jolyon boomed, he had left his spectacles at home and could not read the programme.

'Crusoe's Holiday Island', Lady Phyllis replied, fishing a rustling paper bag containing toffees out of her enormous handbag. 'Now have a toffee Jolyon, the curtain is going up.'

The audience were really enjoying the production. A heavily bearded Bert Biggers was unrecognisable as Robinson Crusoe and Jimmy Griggs as Man Friday, covered in fake dark tan, oil and not much else, was a remarkable sight. Keith Fowler's Ugly Sister was funny and provoked much laughter however, Madge played her Ugly Sister more like Hamlet's mother, full of tragedy and moaning, this was not her finest hour and drew hissing and boos from the audience.

Miranda Fowler's legs in tights calmed things down and Pixie Dean as Dorothy not only danced and sang, but also accompanied herself on the Banjo.

Joe Pickering stomped about proclaiming, 'Fe-foe-fi-fum.' before unfortunately falling off his stilts.

Henri, as Long John Silver arrived in a stage boat with Bluey firmly on his shoulder.

'Pieces of Eight,' Bluey said on cue, he was thankfully being very good, as he really liked Henri, who stroked him when it was time for his line.

Betsy Rowe as Peter Pan did fly, however, unfortunately the wire stuck halfway across the stage and she spent most of the second half dangling above the action.

Cinders or Sophia Mobs had a scene sitting on a stage log with Long John Silver. She was supposed to be telling him how Aladdin was actually a Prince in disguise and pleading for two places on his Pirate ship to take them back to civilisation.

Bluey leaned over from Henri's shoulder and shrieked. 'Kiss me Sophia, I love you'. Repeated over and over again. Sophia burst into tears and ran off the stage. Henri with Bluey still in needle-stuck mode, ran after her. May Bush jumped up shouting, 'So that is what has been going on, I should have guessed'.

The finale was forgotten and the curtain came down.

'I didn't understand the ending, did you Phyllis?' Sir Jolyon remarked as they made their way out of the hall.'

'Hmm, I think there has been more romance going on with the players than in the pantomime.' Lady Phyllis sniffed, adding ruefully. 'Oh what it is to be young.'

Spotting a devastated Phoebe by the entrance, Lady Phyllis gripped her hand. 'Wonderful effort my dear, do congratulate your players, enjoy your after-show party.'

'The party has been cancelled,' an ashen-faced Phoebe muttered, 'I will never work with a parrot ever again'.

Next day the bar of the King's Arms public house was abuzz with gossip about Henri and Sophia. They had run off together and May Bush had decamped back to her London flat. Weeks later the World's press reported that Henri Osman was to star in a Hollywood movie with a new leading lady called Sophia Silver, a recent discovery destined for stardom.

Harry still had his Sunday lunch; however, his granddaughter Jessica now cooked it. A disgraced Bluey was on the waggon and no longer had his tot of rum. This unfortunately increased his bad language and Harry had to close his front door as his neighbours complained.

Artist in Residence

After May Bush and Henri moved out of Foxley Grange it stood empty for several months. Then the "LET BY" sign was erected in the front garden and the usual speculation started.

It wasn't until a dapper figure in a striped blazer and cream straw hat with a matching striped hat band, was seen out walking his dog, and turning into the drive of Foxley Grange that the penny dropped. 'I am sure that is Rollo Barnes, the famous Art historian, Painter, Sculptor and television personality.' An excited Madge reported.

Madge then started exercising her two Chihuahua dogs called Boomps and Daisy in that vicinity, hoping to bump into Rollo. After a few fruitless walks, they did bump into each other or their dogs did.

Picasso, the dog that Rollo had rescued while on a painting trip to Cadaques in Spain was a noisy animal that did not so much bark as have a barking fit. Rollo thought Picasso was wonderful and they were never apart.

The two Chihuahuas were of an extremely nervous disposition and when they saw and heard Picasso barking as he trotted beside Rollo, they shook themselves into a blur.

'Hello, what a lovely dog you have'. Madge lied, 'what breed is he?'

Rollo stopped and smiled, 'Yes Picasso is of a very unusual strain. I am never quite sure who his parents were as I found him abandoned in Spain and named him after

Picasso, the artist. Picasso was one of many famous artists who painted there.' Madge returned his smile thinking; a mongrel is a mongrel however much you love them. However, she bent down and patted Picasso. This provoked more barking and messy hand licking for her trouble.

'Oh, he likes you, how nice.' Rollo said, 'what is your name?'

'My name is Madge Kenton, and I live in Little Humpton, not far from here. Your face is very familiar, have I seen you on the television?'

Rollo sighed; it was hard to be just one of the crowd once you were on television. 'Yes I am on the box rather a lot. Art and quizzes, that sort of thing.'

'How lovely,' Madge gushed, 'we really do need a bit of culture round here. It would be such a joy if you would be able to start an art class in the village.'

'That sounds a good idea to me.' Rollo could never resist flattery, and Madge was laying it on with a trowel.

Madge already visualised herself as an elegant soiree hostess. 'Let me ask around and get back to you, Have you a card Mr Barnes?'

'Oh, please call me Rollo, I have just rented Foxley Grange so it is a bit early for cards, but do drop by when you are passing.'

'Wonderful, so glad we met Rollo.' Madge picked up her whimpering dogs, one under each arm, and made her way back to Little Humpton.

It turned out there were many would be daubers in Little and Greater Humpton, and after checking with Rollo a timetable was agreed. There would be ten sessions on a Thursday evening in the village hall with the promise of a famous guest artist as well. Twelve villagers with their paints and drawing materials arrived and Madge introduced Rollo with glowing praise.

'We are so lucky to have such a famous artist in our midst, let us hope some of his magic will rub off on us. Over to you Rollo.'

'Thank you, Mrs Kenton, or may I call you Madge?' Rollo's old world manners were a joy to Madge, who smiled round at the assembled class. 'First I will give you a short talk on the types of material we will use. Then we will have a life drawing session.' Rollo said, opening his notes.

Puzzled faces were turned towards him. Jimmy Griggs whispered, 'Does that mean we will be drawing someone who is in the buff?'

'I hope not, 'a terrified Fanny Jones said, 'I have only ever seen my husband with nothing on, and that was after we were married'.

Everyone sat down behind the long trestle tables that were usually used for the Scouts jumble sales or sausage and mash quiz nights. They had all seen and heard Rollo Barnes on the television and found it quite riveting being in his class. When Rollo finished his initial talk, there was a stunned silence as he pulled back a curtain on the stage, and revealed a naked Joan Balcombe seated on a shawl draped, wicker chair.

Joan and her husband Howard were nudists and entertained friends from their nudist club behind the high brick garden wall that surrounded their bungalow in Greater Humpton. They also spent most of the summer in the Greek Islands. This was obvious as there were no white patches in Joan's all over tan.

Harry Mobs was peering at the bare-all Joan, and produced his stronger glasses as he could not believe what he was seeing. He had only been recruited at the last minute to make up the numbers to the required dozen. The sweet Sophia Silver, formerly Mobs, had ordered and paid for his art materials on the internet. Harry now had the best equipment of them all.

Towards the end of the session, Joe Pickering made the excuse of needing a toilet break in order to go outside for a crafty cigarette. As Joe opened the door, Picasso who had been left outside the Hall saw his chance and dashed in and up on to the stage, landing on a startled Joan. Jumping up, Joan ran off and did not stop until she reached the safety of her bungalow and Howard.

Joan was of ample proportions and in her haste to escape from Picasso, she had not stopped for her shawl to cover her embarrassment, the class sat transfixed that so much could wobble.

Fred Constable, on duty at the Police station received several phone calls reporting a streaker in the village. He went out with his torch but found nothing; however, he was not pleased, as he had to spend two hours on a report regarding the incident for Head Office.

Picasso was caught and tethered outside, and the class resumed. Rollo pinned every drawing up round the room and looked at them carefully, managing to say something nice about each one. When he came to Harry's large drawing of Joan, he and everyone could not believe how good it was. 'I think this is definitely your subject Harry, your understanding of the curves and hollows of the human body is masterful.'

Unfortunately, Harry who had left his deaf aid at home had no idea what Rollo was saying but he knew it was favourable. 'Can we do the same thing again next week?' Harry asked.

'No, I think we will tackle the painting of fruit next.' Rollo replied, realising Joan would not be returning. My dear friend Clarissa Sparks is coming to stay so perhaps I can persuade---,' there was a pause as Rollo was unsure how to continue. 'So we will be in for a treat.' he concluded.

There was an excited buzz as Clarissa was a well-known artist, famous for fruit and flower drawings and for being in the gossip columns. Sometimes appearing in a dress as Clarissa and sometimes in male attire as Clarence.

'If you ask me,' Drusilla remarked to anyone who would listen, 'it is done merely to hike up the price of his quite ordinary daubs.' Drusilla was very sniffy about this sort of thing.

The following Thursday, Rollo turned up with Clarissa. The whole class arrived early; this was too good to miss. Clarissa wore a pink flowery dress with a pink straw hat and gold sandals. Her make-up was extreme, all blue eye shadow and orange lipstick. When she spoke, her voice danced from a high squeak to a deep baritone. However, as she drew a bunch of cherries on a white board everyone craned forward in admiration. The brush strokes were tiny and the dark and light reds made the fruit look real.

'Brilliant,' Rollo remarked, 'thank you, Clarissa. Now you can all have a go at painting a bunch of cherries or whatever I give you, yourself.' He then distributed an item of fruit to everyone. Clarissa did the rounds helping the class, an extra line here a stronger colour there. Soon they all forgot what an extraordinary sight Clarissa was.

The star pupil this week was Madge. As she said 'I spend so much time gardening I could draw fruit and vegetables in my sleep. Can I have a word to the class please Rollo?'

Rollo nodded and Madge, keen to introduce a Soiree event, invited everyone to a garden party on the Saturday of the next weekend. 'Of course you and Clarissa are invited.' she said.

'Thank you, Madge, unfortunately I will not be able to attend,' Clarissa said, 'however, Clarence would love to be there.'

'Well he will be very welcome.' a bemused Madge said, with her best "learnt at finishing school" type smile.

On the Saturday, which luckily was a bright and sunny day, Rollo arrived with Clarence. It was the same person that had been at the Art class but now dressed in a grey linen suit and purple knitted tie. On his head was a black velvet beret.

Madge had laid on an excellent buffet in her large garden and had briefed the local Humpton newspaper on how two famous artists would be visiting. In the next edition of the paper, there was a photo on the front page of Madge laughing with Rollo and Clarence.

The headline read. "Madge Kenton entertains Art Royalty."

It was well worth the twenty pounds she had dropped the young reporter, Madge thought as she pinned a framed copy up in her downstairs cloakroom.

Doctors' Orders

There was a new, and very keen Doctor who had taken over the local Practice when old Doctor Palmer retired and moved to Portugal to improve his Golf. The Practice was in Little Humpton, but covered both Little and Greater Humpton, and included Waddlington Major.

Doctor Tang was of Chinese extraction but had been born and educated in the Home Counties. He had won over all the female patients when they first went to see him by being amazed when he looked at their particulars.

'I cannot believe the age I am reading here, you look at least ten years younger.' He would say with a smile, and so unsurprisingly they all remarked how lovely they found the new Doctor.

Doctor Tang was a very modern Doctor who believed in keeping weight down and lots of exercise. He proved his point by being in great shape himself, and had been a rowing blue and star footballer when at University.

Lady Phyllis Chudleigh had a bit of a wheezy chest, so had made an appointment to see Doctor Tang. When the Doctor stood up to welcome her she towered over him by at least eight inches.

'How can I help?' the Doctor enquired, quickly sitting down behind his desk, and for once not going through his age reduction ploy.

'I cannot get rid of this rotten cough Doctor, just give me some linctus or some new-fangled cough medicine.

Jolyon says he is fed up with my coughing waking him up at night.'

'Hmm, please undo your cardigan,' Doctor Tang said getting out his stethoscope. 'Nothing serious,' he reported after a quick circuit round Lady Phyllis's ample chest, 'I will give you some antibiotic medicine and you just need to lose about three stone in weight.'

'What?' she boomed indignantly, 'I have been this weight all my life and you are the first person to suggest that I am overweight'.

Doctor Tang smiled, thinking, no surprise there, only a medical man would dare mention it.

'Well the current weight chart reads, that for your height you should be three stones less. Now do you do any sport?' He smiled at Lady Phyllis who had succumbed to a fit of coughing.

'I used to ride to hounds until some idiot do-gooders stopped that. Also, I am Captain of the Ladies' Bowls team'.

Doctor Tang looked ecstatic. 'Well there you are. Just take your medicine, cut down on the cakes, puddings and biscuits and get out on that Bowling Green. Come and see me in a month's time.'

With that, Lady Phyllis went off clutching her prescription. Later she reported to Sir Jolyon that the new Doctor was a midget with a weight phobia.

Everyone who visited the Surgery received the same advice, less indulgence and more exercise. Villagers could not look out of their front windows without seeing someone sweating and puffing as they jogged past. The sale of trainers escalated, much to the delight of the owner of the General Store in Greater Humpton. Swanking posts appeared on younger folk's Facebook pages, 'Did two point three miles today' followed by several smiley faces. The most sought after birthday present was one of those watches that measured how far you had jogged. Even old Harry Mobs dragged himself out of his chair and limped to the Pub, receiving a cheer as he entered.

The Humpton Ladies' Bowls Club had been the first club with female members in England, and was still run according to the original rules. These specified, "No jewellery, no bare legs, no trousers, only white pleated skirts, white blouses, official blazers and hats with hatbands to be allowed".

'How alluring am I?' Gasped Miranda Fowler in horror when she tried on her new uniform in the master bedroom of 'The Fowlery', a cute name she had devised for the detached house she and Keith shared in Little Humpton.

'Very'. Leered Keith, making a lunge for her. Ever since Matron at boarding school, he had harboured a weakness for females in uniform.

'Stop it Keith, I haven't time for that now'. Miranda admonished, rushing out. She did not want to be late on her first day at the Club.

The Ladies' Clubhouse was situated between Little and Greater Humpton. There were actually two Clubhouses as the Men's Clubhouse faced it, with the two Greens between and a low hedge dividing them. Both sexes were forbidden to fraternize, apart from when the men were invited to a special afternoon tea that took place at the end of the season. Otherwise, even husbands and wives were not supposed to acknowledge each other.

When Miranda had parked her car in the members' car park, she entered the clubhouse and cannoned into Lady Phyllis.

'What do I do first?' she enquired nervously.

'How about good morning and please excuse me for bumping into you Lady Phyllis?' Phyllis was a stickler for good manners.

'Oops sorry Lady Phyllis, I am all at sea today, I only just made it out of the house.' Miranda giggled in her little girl way, leaving the others wondering what she was talking about.

'This is your locker dear and this is the rota for tea duty on the notice board.' Lady Phyllis, whose bark was worse than her bite, said kindly, indicating first the green locker with a key in it and then a long list of names and dates. 'We all do a week when we get the afternoon tea and then wash up afterwards.'

Miranda looked at her long painted nails and did not like the sound of that. Washing up were not two words with which she was familiar. However, she smiled at Lady Phyllis and then studied the rota intently.

'Wonderful', she breathed, determined to be a team player.

Out on the Green, Miranda was put in a team with Madge, Daisy and Fanny. They were playing a team skippered by Lady Phyllis. Contrary to most rules, Lady

Phyllis had brought along Tingaling who acted as her runner. Rushing around excitedly every time a wood landed near the jack and fetching those that had landed in the ditch. Unfortunately, Tingaling's knowledge of the game was rudimentary and she would retrieve woods that were in the right place.

'This foreign person spoils the game'. a furious Madge declared after her last wood landed right next to the jack, and was brought back by a smiling Tingaling.

'Well our team won anyway, so let us have tea now'. Lady Phyllis said, and swept back to the clubhouse, leaving Tingaling to put the bowls in her bag and collect the mat and jack.

'What a shambles, I am going to make a complaint about that Tingaling.' Madge snorted as she led her defeated team back.

'Oh, Tingaling really loves helping, if you complain Madge, I will put it down to racial prejudice.'

Madge knew when she was beaten, so decided to shelve the Bowls Club for a while and think of something else to channel her energy into, and so be in the good books of Doctor Tang.

Tingaling had become a firm favourite with Lady Phyllis who was fascinated with all things oriental. Every morning before Sir Jolyon stirred; Lady Phyllis and Tingaling could be found on the lawn of Frogitt Hall with a wind up 'His Masters Voice' gramophone, going through the movements of Tai Chi. This was to the strains of Jeanette McDonald and Nelson Eddy singing the Indian Love Call.

The record was very scratched but they found it conducive to the movements and mood. Tingaling was now in charge. Lady Phyllis's bones were not as supple as the much younger Tingaling however, they both enjoyed these early morning sessions enormously.

The Nature Walk

Back home a disgruntled Madge decided to give Bowls a rest and to start a Nature Walk instead. This would begin by the church in Little Humpton; go over the Common, to the Fen then along the riverbank, past Greater Humpton village, finishing up at The Hind Public House for lunch. This was quite a step but luckily, there was a small train run by local enthusiasts on Saturdays. It ran between the villages and Madge decided that the group would come back on that, making it only a one-way walk.

Madge had put a notice up in the General Store and had received a somewhat tepid response, but with her usual enthusiasm she had strong-armed the number up to eight. On the first Saturday, their numbers would be swelled by Rosie her niece, and Jed, Rosie's boyfriend who happened to be staying with Madge that week. Madge was not very keen on them visiting but could not think of a reason to refuse when her sister Annie had phoned to say they were dying to see her.

'More like Annie is tired of them hanging around the house and wants to get rid of them.' Madge confided to Drusilla who had popped in for a cup of coffee. 'Rosie was a lovely little girl but now all she wants to do is smooch with this Jed. I just don't understand girls anymore. What is this obsession Rosie has to wash her hair every morning? Also, she is a nightmare to feed as she says she is allergic to nearly everything I have in the cupboard. Fish, pork, eggs, wheat you name it and she says, "That will make me spotty and ill." 'When I was growing up we ate everything that we were given.'

'Never mind Madge, we will go to the Pub before we catch the train back and she can have air pie and we will stuff ourselves rotten.'

'That will defeat the object Drusilla'. Madge said sternly, 'according to our lovely new Doctor we are supposed to be bringing our weight down, however, they do really nice food in The Hind, so I may be tempted.'

Drusilla stirred her coffee thoughtfully, 'Did you once tell me that your sister's husband was a right pain?'

'I did and he is,' Madge replied. 'What possessed Annie to marry Evans the Car I will never know? Oh sorry that is confusing. Actually, his name is Hugh, but he came from a mining village and started out selling cars from the front of his mother's cottage. He did well and now he has a large dealership in the Midlands. He is the rudest man I have ever met and why Annie stays with him is a mystery. I think Annie likes the money and lifestyle he offers. Hugh's only conversation is about cars, otherwise he just sits there like a glowering dummy.' Madge paused for breath.

'I gather you don't like him,' said Drusilla, stating the obvious.

'Well he has caused no end of trouble in our family, and delights in trying to drive a wedge between my sister and me. I put it down to an inferiority complex due to his humble beginnings. Annie came down here with Rosie and Jed, dumped them on me and hardly said a word, then drove back immediately. I had a feeling that she had a pressing engagement.'

'That is odd, do you suspect a little love interest situation?' Drusilla was a great one for romance and was never without a magazine containing true love stories.

'Goodness gracious! I had not thought of that however, I would not blame Annie if she did stray. I mean, Rosie is off to University in September and Annie will get an attack of empty- nest syndrome.'

Drusilla looked at her watch. 'Gosh look at the time I really must fly, lots to do. Roll on Saturday, I will meet you outside the church at ten sharp. Good luck with your visitors.' With that, she kissed Madge and squeezed her hand. 'Don't let Evans the Car get you down.'

'Thanks darling,' Madge replied, 'one more nasty thing out of him and he's toast.'

At ten o'clock outside Little Humpton Church Madge counted heads. It was a full turnout plus Rosie and Jed. 'Good Morning every one, so glad you could all make it. If you are ready let us be on our way, now try and keep together.' With that, they set off in pairs, Madge leading with Fred Constable who was an expert on birds, followed by Keith Fowler who had three cameras and several long lenses strapped around him. Miranda Fowler trotted beside him, a vision in pink, pink shorts, pink anorak, pink trainers and a pink sunhat. Next, came Drusilla and Pixie Dean each carrying a book on wild flowers, then Daisy and Bert Biggers. Daisy had dragged Bert along with the promise of the super food, plus a beer at The Hind Public House.

Bringing up the rear were Rosie and Jed. They had wanted to stay behind but Madge was not allowing that and was quite firm. 'I want you where I can see you.' She said as she shushed them out of the house. However, every time they came to a building or some trees the pair would lag behind until someone would be dispatched to round them up.

The Common proved to have some quite exotic flowers growing amongst the tufts of grass and dandelions. Drusilla and Pixie consulted their books. 'Those pink ones with spikes of flowers are Pyramid Orchids and quite rare,' they announced, 'and the others with brown and yellow middles are Bee Orchids and are very rare.'

'Fascinating' Madge enthused noting it down in the logbook she was carrying. 'Now carry on and let's see what else we find.'

As they crossed the road to the Fen, a yellow wagtail ran across their path. Keith Fowler immediately raised his biggest camera to get a shot of it while Fred Constable flagged down an approaching tractor.

'Hold on a minute please.' Fred said to the driver, who happened to be a farmer called Robbie, and the worst tempered man in the county. 'I hate Twitchers,' Robbie shouted, 'stopping a man doing an honest day's work. If you don't move that man I will run him over and the blinking bird.'

'You better not or I will take down you particulars.' Even though Fred was off duty, he could not forget that he was the strong arm of the Law.

Keith by now had the photo he wanted and the whole group crossed the road while a still cursing Robbie trundled away.

Yellow Wagtail, Madge noted in her book, just as a pair of Curlews rose from the ground with their haunting call. Their nest was a shallow depression in the ground lined with plant fragments and contained four pale green eggs with purple blotches. 'This is wonderful.' Keith was ecstatic, snapping away, while Madge's pencil was a blur. Everyone crowded round apart from Rosie and Jed who only had eyes for each other. Suddenly Rosie let out a scream. As she had bent down to pick a buttercup, an insect on it had stung her hand.

'I need to go to Hospital.' Rosie cried, waving her hand aloft.

'Nonsense, come here I have some cream for bites.' Madge, who was always prepared for anything, as she had once been a Girl Guide, produced a First Aid Kit and applied bite cream and a bandage saying. 'Now don't make a fuss darling.'

With Rosie still complaining they walked on. A swarm of flies circled round Jed's head, attracted by his hair gel. It looked as if he had a moving Afro haircut.

'Country life is horrible I wish we could go home.' He whispered to Rosie, who was already on her mobile phone texting her father and begging to be rescued.

The Fen had produced not only many wild flowers and birds but also some interesting animals. Rabbits, field mice and a couple of voles.

A lone kestrel hovered over his prey while a pheasant took off with whirring wings, and an explosive cry like jangling tin cans. Madge turned a page in her notebook as they reached the riverbank.

A flash of brilliant blue was a Kingfisher flying along above the river, while further upstream a Heron took off with slow flapping wings and trailing long legs.

It had begun to rain and suddenly everyone apart from Rosie and Jed had whipped out a plastic mac and put them on. 'Can we go back, Auntie Madge?' Whimpered Rosie.

'Definitely not, a little bit of rain never hurt anyone. Now show what you are made of Rosie. It is only a shower.'

And so, it proved, the sun came out just as the pub came into view.

The Hind was the sort of place Americans love, and very 'Merrie Old England' looking. Madge ushered her party in and they found tables and seats in the Bar. The Landlord was expecting them so while the men ordered the drinks, the others studied the menu chalked on the blackboards by the Bar.

All the walking had made them hungry apart from Rosie who asked for just a diet Coke. Everyone else chose from a variety of dishes. Steak and Ale pie, Sausage and mash, Chicken in a basket, Baked Potato with fillings and Ploughman's with French bread. While they waited for their food to arrive they all compared their notes and tried to understand their hasty scribble.

The food as predicted was delicious. Jed managed most of his Ploughman's while Rosie just tapped away on her phone.

Pixie nudged Daisy. 'What do they find to say?'

'Search me', Daisy replied as she attacked her pie with relish, and raised her glass of red wine. But it can't beat a glass of plonk whatever they say.'

The train station was next to the pub, and half an hour later they all lined up as the train chugged into the tiny station, steam rising up from its funnel and the smell of burning coal wafting from the hot cab. A loud hoot and whistle from the driver, and then the guard shouted, 'All aboard.'

There was a scramble as Madge made sure all her party had seats, the guard blew his whistle and they were off on their way back to Little Humpton.

When they arrived back at the village, everyone thanked Madge for a fun day out, apart from Jed and Rosie who were in a silent clinch.

'Thank you all for coming, now write up your notes and we will compile a piece for the Humpton News.' Madge smiled, thinking well that was a triumph if I say so myself and then loaded the silent lovers into her car for the short journey back to her house.

As she drove up there was a vast 4 by 4 parked on the drive. Madge pulled up behind it and got out.

'Hugh what are doing here?'

'I have come to take my daughter home as you are causing her great distress, and before she comes to any more harm. You are a danger to anyone and completely heartless, no wonder your husband died young.' Hugh's thin voice was cold with venom.

That did it, Madge was ablaze with anger. Years of having to bite back what she wanted to say were over.

'How dare you, you pathetic excuse for a man. I have spent years trying to ignore all your insulting behaviour but if you bring my late husband into it, that is the final straw, I will never speak to you again. Now take your daughter and never darken my doorstep again.'

A terrified Rosie and Jed ran to Hugh's car and got in. Rosie then remembered her belongings, opening the car window she shouted. 'Auntie my things'.

In no mood to calm down, Madge said coldly, 'Get old money bags to buy you new ones, now get off my land.'

As they drove away, Madge went back into her house and was greeted by her two yappy Chihuahuas; she then went straight to her Cocktail cabinet. There were times when only a glass of Sherry was what the doctor ordered, and this was one of them. Ten minutes later, she phoned her sister.

Annie answered and was not surprised by the tale of a fracas with Hugh.

'I was out, but Rosie had sent me a text full of tales of how unhappy she was staying in the sticks, as she put it. I know she is a pain and I hope that university will toughen her up.'

'Well I know she is my niece but I had quite enough of her and Jed so I am not sorry she has gone. Hugh and I had words and I told him I never want to see him again.' Madge was prepared for her sister springing to the defence of Hugh, but to her surprise Annie said, 'So have I. When I got back from bringing Rosie to you I caught Hugh red handed with his secretary. I thought something was going on, and that was why I rushed back. We are going to divorce and I am so relieved. He is a real pain and she is welcome to him.'

Madge let out a gasp of surprise thinking; I thought it would be the other way around. How could anyone fancy that excuse for a human being. However, she just said, 'Well I can't say I'm sorry. Keep in touch and you are always welcome to stay if you want to get away.'

'Thanks,' Annie said, sounding tearful. 'I may take you up on that. Goodbye big sister.'

'Fancy that'. Madge said to the dogs as she hung up the phone and poured herself another large Sherry. 'There are times when only getting a bit squiffy will do, and today was one of them.'

Dancing and Dating

As summer drifted into autumn, several changes happened in the villages. First Rollo Barnes left Foxley Grange. He was approached by an Arts Foundation to set up an Exhibition in Spain and found the offer irresistible.

'It is right up my street figuratively speaking.' He had said to Thomas Perkins when he went to the Letting Agency to terminate his tenancy. 'I have really enjoyed living here but I cannot turn down this chance. '

Thomas had to agree, as he would swap living in Greater Humpton for Spain at the drop of a hat.

'Of course, the apartment that goes with the job is not a patch on Foxley Grange, however, some of my best times were in shacks.' Rollo continued with a shrug as Thomas laughed.

'We will miss you, your art classes were a huge success.' Thomas added, already wondering to whom he could let the property.

'Well I am taking some of Harry Mobs's drawings of nudes to hang beside some by famous artists like Picasso and Dali. How Harry acquired such a feeling for the female form is a mystery.'

Thomas nodded, thinking perhaps there was some truth in the rumours that had swirled round the village about Harry and his Home Helps.

A rather large lady and a man in a wheelchair arrived at Foxley Grange, and the village drums went into overdrive. The lady was an Agony Aunt on television called

Dee Bee, not her real name, but thought up by the 'suits' at the studios. The man in the wheelchair was her boyfriend, who had been a modern dance champion until he had fallen while hoisting his dance partner aloft, and had badly injured his back.

Madge, never one to let the grass grow under her feet, dropped a card through their letterbox inviting Dee Bee round for coffee. A couple of days later Dee emailed her acceptance and finally arrived after several attempts to find the right house.

'Gosh,' she puffed as Madge opened the front door, 'I had a terrible time finding you, the numbers all start the wrong way round.'

'I know,' Madge acknowledged, 'unfortunately the chap that built these houses was dyslexic and the numbers do not make much sense. Now you have found me do come in, I'm so glad you are here.'

Madge recognised Dee from her appearances on Day Time Television where she had a weekly advice slot; she also did radio talk shows and wrote a column in a monthly magazine. The curly blonde permed hair and Northern accent were unmistakable.

'I do so admire your down to earth approach to problems.' Madge said as she ushered Dee into her large morning room. 'Now do you like cream or milk with your coffee? And can I tempt you to one of my homemade scones?'

Dee settled into the deep chintzy luxury of Madge's large sofa and sipped her coffee.

'I understand your partner has had a most unfortunate accident and is in a wheelchair.' Madge ventured, having seen this mentioned in the gossip columns.

'Yes, Alain was the star dancer on the celebrity dance programme, but sustained a bad back injury when his lady dance partner fell heavily on him during a lift. He is very frustrated and is trying to practise in his wheelchair, although it is hard to find an area big enough even in a big house like Foxley Grange.'

Madge made clucking sympathetic noises saying. 'I do so hope he recovers soon, I love that programme.' Even though it was something she never watched.

Soon they were like old friends and Madge found herself telling Dee about her sister Annie's recent marriage split.

'It sounds like that was a break up waiting to happen. I would like to meet your sister. Oh just one more then they are delicious.' Dee said as Madge offered her another scone.

'Annie is coming to stay in a couple of weeks; I would love you to meet her, as I think she is a trifle lost at the minute.'

'Understandable, the best thing she can do is move on. Have you ever held a Speed Dating night in the village?'

'Speed dating?' Madge had a vague idea of what that entailed although there had never been such a thing in either Little, or Greater Humpton.

'Right, I will help you organise one if you can find a suitable venue. I can feature it on the local radio.' Dee was nothing if not positive, and her permed curls shook with excitement. Nothing pleased her more than matchmaking.

'A very nice lady and an asset to our village,' Madge said, when she approached the caretaker of the village hall to open the bar and provide some alcohol on that night. 'Just to ease the wheels a bit and get things moving.'

Annie had arrived for her visit, and somewhat reluctantly agreed to attend the Speed Dating night on the following Friday.

'What do I do?' she asked Dee when they met on the night of the event

'Well, you wear this name badge and a number, you will have 5 minutes with each male and if you would like to see him again circle his name. If you both want to make contact, I will inform you the next day. Oh, and you give yourself a pseudonym, not your real name then write it on this blank badge.'

Annie sat at one of the small tables set out with some sheets of paper, a bottle of wine and two glasses in the centre. As the hall filled up Annie tried to think of a suitable name and came up with Girl Friday. After all, she was a girl and it was Friday.

Precisely at eight o'clock Dee rang her bell, and then noticed that they were a lady short. 'Madge, can you fill in please? Or else someone will have to leave.'

Madge hastily pinned on a badge, never one to let the side down.

There was a mixed bunch of familiar faces from the local villages. Also, some unfamiliar ones who had obviously heard Dee's broadcast. The ages were a wide spread from mid-twenties to what one would say were perhaps approaching a midlife crisis   Amazingly, amongst them was Professor William Wolfe, the historian from Waddlington Major. Although no one knew, he had long harboured a sneaking regard for Madge. He liked strong women with a touch of vinegar.

Dee blew her whistle and the first five minutes ticked away. Some were tongue-tied, and some over-egged the pudding. However, as the contents of the bottles on the tables decreased, the level of the noise revved up and laughter bounced round the walls.

On the fifth blast from Dee's whistle, William arrived at the table occupied by Madge.

'I am surprised to see you here Professor.' Madge said, as she poured herself another glass of wine and topped his up.

'Well endless dusty research can be very lonely and I would like a lady to take out for meals and to the theatre.'

Madge stared at him in a new light, she had never really thought of him in that way.

'I know what you mean, I would like what they call 'a walker' for such things. However,' She looked pointedly at his whiskers.

The professor got the point. 'If you put a ring round my name I will shave off my beard.'

Madge smiled and her pencil did just that.

Annie enjoyed the evening and several men had ringed her name but as she said to Madge and Dee I really have had enough of male company after years with Hugh, now I love being alone and doing just what I want. I am going to take up loads of hobbies and sports to find different outlets. Also, I am planning a long Cruise to the other side of The World. Being here with you both has been an enormous help and clarified in my mind what to do after my divorce.'

Several couples did find people they would like to see again. Dee decided to make this a monthly event and told her listeners all about the next date for Speed Dating.

Alain who was very frustrated at not being able to practice his dance moves in the house, decided to use the frozen pond in the garden of Foxley Grange. A sudden cold snap due to winds blowing down from the Arctic had caused sheets of thick ice to form on the surface of the large pond. When Dee was out, he whirled his wheelchair around while humming relevant tunes. Rumbas, Tangos, Quicksteps, they all could be tackled on the ice.

This was fine until the temperatures went up and the ice began to melt, although it still looked able to take the weight of Alain and his wheelchair. As he executed the intricate swirls of the Viennese Waltz in the middle of the pond there was a loud crack. Both he and the wheelchair went through the ice, and both were partially submerged.

Luckily, a few minutes later the Postman was doing his daily delivery and heard faint cries coming from the back garden as he went to put the day's mail through the letterbox. When he saw Alain in the icy water, he immediately phoned Emergency, realising it would take several people to rescue Alain, who had already turned a very funny colour with distinctly blue lips.

In a matter of minutes, a big yellow helicopter could be heard approaching, and it landed in the garden. Two burly medics jumped out and the three of them got Alain out of the pond. A minute later, he was wrapped in a tin foil blanket and on his way to hospital.

When Dee heard what had happened she rushed to his bedside and was told that apart from hypothermia Alain was in good shape. In fact, the jolt as he entered the water had put his spine back to its proper place and cured the injury. He spent several days in the hospital while Dee took to the airwaves to say how wonderful the Rescue Service had been, and that the Postman deserved a medal. A petition was started and when there were thousands of signatures, it was delivered by Dee to number 10 Downing Street, London.

The Non-Boot, Boot Sale

Lady Phyllis was thrilled when the rescue helicopter landed and took Alain off to Hospital. However, she was aghast to learn that it was all paid for by funds raised by donations.

'We must do our bit.' She said to the ladies of the village reading circle when they met at Frogitt Hall. 'Now what suggestions have you to raise money for this worthy cause?'

After ten minutes of quite heated debate, it was agreed to hold a Boot Sale but without the cars and therefore without the Boots or Trunks, Lady Phyllis added trunks to show how cosmopolitan she was.

'We can use the two big barns we have behind the Hall, and perhaps we can have some sort of hot refreshment outside to warm the crowd up, bearing in mind that this is winter.' As usual, Lady Phyllis was full of enthusiasm once she had an idea to kick around.

'Gluvine and Stollen.' Chirped Miranda, she and Keith had just returned from a coach tour of the Christmas Markets in Germany.

'Good idea Miranda, and we can get Busby to do hot chestnuts, he has done that before. Now I will organise the posters and the set-up here with Tingaling, and you can all go round the villages and get any Bric-a-brac that we can sell' Lady Phyllis smiled round as all the ladies filed out chattering excitedly. Miranda, especially glowing at being praised.

The Saturday of the Sale was cold but dry. The barns luckily, had electricity installed in them and were warm and welcoming. The really big one had trestle tables with numerous diverse objects piled up high on them. The other barn contained a range of cars that Sir Jolyon kept long after anyone drove them. Busby looked after them as if they were his own and could often be found polishing them even on his days off.

Pride of place was Sir Jolyon's Phantom Rolls Royce; it was silver with pale leather upholstery. Beside it was a Lagonda drop head coupe, once owned by Sir Jolyon's racy aunt, the Hon. Myra Chudleigh. Looking a bit dwarfed by these bigger models was the Morris Minor 1000 or jelly mould as it was called affectionately. It had been the car that Lady Phyllis would drive at breakneck speed round the surrounding villages to do her good works. An ancient pre-war Rover 12 with the number plate CGP 944, was kept because those were the initials of Charles George Plantagenet, an uncle of Jolyon's, now sadly departed. A lovely blaze red M G B with metal bumpers and wire wheels, and lastly a black T R 7 with pop-up headlights completed the line-up.

A nonstop crowd filed past the cars as if they were royalty lying in state. Joe Pickering, who was a car buff, answered all their questions, and stopped small children clambering over the exhibits.

The amount of things collected to sell was staggering. Every door in the local villages had been knocked on, and every room, garage and shed had turned up some unwanted item. The ladies of the book club stood behind the tables ready to take the money, and see no one got away without paying.

Outside Keith and Miranda manned a mobile bar made by a member of staff called Plummer. He was Frogitt Hall's outside man, that meant he dealt with anything that was in the grounds of Frogitt Hall. From the gaudily painted bar, the hot Gluvine in plastic cups and slices of Stollen on paper napkins were sold to a never-ending queue. They did a roaring trade while Busby's well used brazier cooked wonderfully smelling chestnuts that popped and crackled. Crowds gathered round enjoying the warmth as they lined up to buy a bag of hot chestnuts.

Inside the shed with the items for sale was a newish inhabitant of Greater Humpton. A tall rakish character called Jake Blake. Quite a few people looked at him, as he was a well-known face from the newspapers and television. His brushes with the law were frequently documented. Recently he had bought a large rambling house that stood behind tall hedges on three acres of land. It had electric gates and was quite isolated. The papers called him by his popular name of Diamond Jake. This was because of the diamonds embedded in his front teeth that glinted as he spoke.

Towering above the rows of people pawing through the merchandise, Diamond Jake was showing great interest in an old terracotta ornament and was just about to pick it up when Tingaling darted in front of him and grabbed it.

'Sowwy, that is sold.' she said, and was off like a flash carrying the ornament to the Hall.

'What the ----,' Jake said, followed by several swear words.

'Watch your language, ladies present'. Jimmy Griggs, who was standing nearby said, drawing himself up to his full height, his military looking moustache bristling.

'I was just about to buy that when some Chinese lady whipped it away.' Jake shouted in a complaining, angry voice

'It had been sold some time before but left out by mistake'. Jimmy said, realising there must be a reason for Tingaling's sudden intervention.

Jimmy knew all about Jake who was one of five brothers, four of them including Jake had a long list of convictions. The only straight one was Phillip, a Q C who gave his time for free to represent his brothers when their cases came up in Court. Their father had been an opportunist scoundrel and rag and bone man in the original rough East End. After making a fortune, he had moved his family out of London, however, old family traditions run deep and apart from Phillip, the others remained firmly on the wrong side of the law.

When people questioned Thomas as to why he had sold the house to a person with such a dubious reputation, he replied, 'Even villains have to live somewhere.'

When Jimmy caught up with Tingaling inside the Hall, he asked why she had taken the figure away.

'I have seen these Terracotta figures before in China, they are very old and very valuable. I will ask Her Ladyship to find out who it belonged to, and see if they know its real worth.' This was said in Tingaling's garbled, excitable language.

'Good girl,' Jimmy said. 'Leave it in Sir Jolyon's study until he returns.'

At five o'clock Sir Jolyon declared the Non Boot Sale over. As the last customers drifted away and the big clear up began, a little old woman went up to Lady Phyllis with a worried look.

'I gave an old terracotta ornament to the person calling to collect things to sell. When I told my daughter, she says she thinks it could have been valuable'.

Lady Phyllis recognised the woman, a proud but desperately poor widow living in the village.

'Oh dear,' she said but got no further as a very excited Tingaling ran up smiling.

'I save it, nasty man want it but Tingaling run away and put it in Sir's study. It may be worth a lot of money.'

'Well done dear.' Lady Phyllis beamed at Tingaling then turned to the old women. 'Now do you want me to get it valued for you Mrs Murray? If it is valuable, we can get it auctioned. Chinese art prices are going through the roof at the present time.'

Mrs Murray looked ready to collapse at this turn of events. 'Oh please,' she said, 'I nearly threw it in the dustbin the other day, I feel quite weak at the thought.'

'Tingaling, take Mrs Murray up to the Hall and get her a cup of tea. You really are quite an art connoisseur.'

Tingaling was not sure what that meant but hoped it was good. She loved to be in Lady Phyllis's good books.'

The following week, Sir Jolyon contacted the head of a Bond Street auction house and their top expert was dispatched to look at the terracotta ornament. It was indeed, he relayed a genuine ancient artefact. A sale to a private collector for over a million pounds was arranged. Mrs Murray now had enough money to live comfortably for the rest of her life. She and her daughter took a cruise up the European rivers, and she returned looking fit and well. Doctor Tang told her she looked ten years younger.

TV Dinners

Among the morning's post that Busby took into Sir Jolyon's study was a brown envelope with the logo of a well-known T V company in the left hand corner.

'Looks exciting Sir.' Busby said as he put the silver salver containing the letters down on the leather topped desk

'Harrumph, blinking leftie luvies I expect, always wanting me to back their charities. Wouldn't mind but it's mainly to show how caring they are, my money and their self-promotion. You open it for me please Busby, I will take a gander at these others which look like bills, see what trifles Lady Phyllis has spent my dwindling cash on.'

While Sir Jolyon set to work with his pearl handled paper knife, Busby expertly opened the brown envelope and took out the single page letter, then passed it to Sir Jolyon.

After a quick read of the contents, he said to Busby, 'What do you think of that? They want to use the Hall and kitchens for the opening programme of the new TV cooking series with that lady chef, Gloria Creasy-Bull.

Busby let out a low whistle before he could stop himself, 'That is the one they call Greasy- Balls, she tends to wear very low necklines when she vigorously beats her mixtures.'

Sir Jolyon looked thoughtful for a minute. 'Well if you can get Tingaling to approve of an interloper in her territory, I will run it past Lady Phyllis. Personally, as they are offering a tidy sum, I am all for it.'

'Tingaling guards her copper pans as if they are ancient masterpieces by Michelangelo, however, if Lady Phyllis is for it then Tingaling will be'. Busby said, knowing how devoted Tingaling was to Lady Phyllis.

The next week several batches of television manager types arrived at Frogitt Hall with IPads and inspected the facilities, shouting instructions to their assistants to make a note of what was needed. The assistants seemed mainly to be called Adrian, Becky or 'you there'.

Tingaling bristled when they invaded her kitchen and began poking around in her fabulously pristine domain.

'Sooo old fashioned,' a Becky remarked viewing the rows of copper pans hanging in graduated sizes on the wall. 'If it won't go in the dishwasher I wouldn't have it. Have you seen this ancient mixer? The only place for that is in a museum'.

Just then, Lady Phyllis entered and heard the slur on her equipment. 'It was a wedding present when Sir Jolyon and I tied the knot,' she proclaimed in her best far back vowels, 'those blue and white mixers are a collector's item, and the pans have been handed down through the generations.'

Becky blushed. 'I am sorry Lady Phyllis; it's only that Gloria will bring her own equipment, she's lost without things she is familiar with using especially after--.' Becky's voice trailed away while an Adrian in the background sniggered.

The date for the first filming was agreed, and also that it would be live. On that day, several large vans arrived at the Hall, and the occupants' usual peaceful existence was shattered. Wires for the cameras and lights were everywhere. Sir Jolyon retreated to his study, and Lady Phyllis decided to visit Madge, who was dying to hear all about this latest event.

'You must let me meet Gloria,' Madge said, 'I have all her books, they are hardly ever out of my hands, her recipes are so easy to follow. And do try and get near to her, and see if she has had any work done.'

'Work?' queried Lady Phyllis. 'What sort of work?'

Madge sighed; Lady Phyllis was not interested in the same things that coloured Madge's existence.

Madge put her fingers each side of her face and pulled the skin up to her ears. 'Face lifts, Botox, that sort of thing.'

Lady Phyllis snorted, 'Good Lord, who wants that? "Never guild the lily", my father, Lord Frogitt would say, and my mother always said "stay away from the knife." Mind you they were no oil paintings themselves.'

'Do you know, I have never seen any portraits of your family at the Hall.' Madge said, settling Lady Phyllis in her large conservatory.

'I have stored them in the attic, no need to frighten visitors.' Lady Phyllis took the cup of tea that Madge had just poured from her Claris Cliff teapot into a matching cup and stared out at the middle-aged man pottering in the garden.

'Thank you, Madge, pretty design. Is that Smith, your new gardener? I heard something about his wife going missing.'

'Yes, a very rum do, Sharon Smith went on a short break with a friend to the Gambia and they never returned. Interpol said they were alive and well but had become engaged to a couple of local lads and were not returning. Naturally, Smith is quite off girls called Sharon, short breaks, and the Gambia is not on his bucket list. Sharon used to do my cleaning as well so I now only have one girl. Sharon was a mixed blessing though as she overcompensated for her lack of brainpower by having a lot of imaginary phobias and allergies. I doubt that her new fiancé will be very tolerant of that sort of thing.

'Now about this Jumble Sale, I have promised the lovely people at the Helicopter Rescue Charity that I would raise some more money if I could. Have you a date I can put to the Village Hall?'

'Not for a month or so Lady Phyllis. I am at the moment running a Novice Gardening Course. I had a huge response from young married ladies anxious to join. In fact, I have a waiting list. Smith is helping me and enjoying telling girls what to do for a change, after the devious Sharon.'

Lady Phyllis finished her tea and put the cup and saucer down on the small glass-topped bamboo table. 'What sort of itinerary do you have for your classes?' An impressed Lady Phyllis asked.

'Well, the girls, six of them, arrive at ten o'clock and we have coffee and a chat. Ten thirty I give an hour's talk on theory, I take that from my gardening magazines. Then practical work in the garden with Smith, weeding, hoeing, trimming, that sort of thing. Then lunch here in the conservatory. More theory for an hour while their lunch goes down, then they finish up with more practical work in the garden with Smith. They enjoy it and so does Smith.'

Lady Phyllis looked out at the garden with a new interest. 'Yes your garden has never looked better, not a weed in sight. Well I must push on; need to check how the run up to the filming is going. I hope Tingaling is not climbing the walls.'

With that, she got up and looked at her watch. 'I will check Gloria for joins, she should have arrived by now and I will phone you later when I know what is happening.'

Back at the Hall, Gloria Creasy-Bull had just arrived with her assistant Grant. She swept in while Grant staggered behind her carrying a mountain of boxes, cookbooks, and followed by Gloria's personal makeup artist, Juno. No one was ever sure if Juno was male or female, although it would be fair to say, neither was Juno.

Gloria was in great shape. A very small waist usually pulled in tightly with a shiny belt and above that, a well-rounded top, very much on display. With her low-cut dresses, one was reminded of rolled beef joints in the Butcher's window. Although not tall, she tottered on vertiginous high-heeled shoes with platform soles. Her blonde hair curled round her shoulders and when she gazed seductively at the camera, she flicked it casually back while she lowered her eyelids and licked her lips.

'Hello, Darlings, well we really have a wonderful place for our first show.' Gloria breathed in her throaty tones. 'Now what am I making today?'

Mary Jane and Jane-Mary her two assistants had everything weighed and measured out on plates and in jugs. 'As we are in a very old country estate we thought you should make something out of Mrs Beeton's book but with a modern twist.'

'Ok so what have we got here?' Gloria said, standing behind the scrubbed wooden table and lifting the covers off two large plates, then recoiling in horror. Underneath were three brace of partridges, complete with feathers, and a rabbit with its fur still in place.

'You stupid girls, what are you up to? I have never fiddled with raw things like this, I usually have nice meat prepared by someone else.'

'But you said you wanted something authentic.' Jane-Mary piped up. 'After Vermicelli Soup, Stewed Rump Steak and Oyster Patties, Mrs Beeton served Curried Rabbit with boiled rice as a second course, followed by Partridges as a third course and then Apple fritters and also-----'

'That's enough'. Gloria screamed, 'you are fired.' Clicking her fingers to the faithful Grant, she added 'medicine Grant quick,'

Grant opened one of the boxes and produced a screw-top bottle of colourless liquid. Gloria snatched it and tipped most of it down the hatch. Then stormed to the door and out into the cobbled kitchen yard shouting over her shoulder, 'Ciggy, Grant quick.'

Delving into another of the boxes he had arrived with, Grant came up with an unopened pack of cigarettes and followed Gloria outside.

Tingaling viewing this with fascinated horror said, 'I am sorry Gloria person fire you.'

'Oh don't worry about that,' the girls chorused, 'Gloria fires us several times a day and then begs us to stay when she sobers up.'

Bruce, the director swore under his breath. 'This is going out live and Gloria, even if she is sober will never prepare those partridges and the rabbit.'

'I can do that, in my country, if it moves we eat it, I will do that no problem.' No problem was Tingaling's favourite saying.

'Can you really do all that on camera? We will film it in advance, and if Gloria is able she will do the rest live.'

'No problem.' Tingaling smiled up at him.

'Great girl. Now if you can start that in the scullery our cameraman will make you a star.'

For the next half hour feathers, fur and guts flew in all directions. Tingaling was in her element. It reminded her of home and while her hands were busy, she talked about the customs and life that she had grown up with in her village.

'My God, what a star!' Bruce said as the cameraman recorded it all on film.

As Tingaling was clearing up, Gloria made a staggering entrance into the kitchen. Bruce's face was registering dismay.

'Right' slurred Gloria, 'have you made those things so I can touch them? What a boring old person that Mrs Beeton must have been, all this roadkill food.'

Holding on to Grant's arm, she staggered to the table and at the sight of the raw jointed rabbit she gasped, 'Bathroom, Grant, quick.'

'Is that Grant Quick her boyfriend?' Tingaling asked, staring after the retreating pair.

'Mary-Jane and Jane-Mary hi-fived and tittered, 'Yes and no' Mary-Jane said, 'Yes it is her boyfriend, and no, his name is Grant Melville. He has a degree in being bossed about.'

'Only kidding Tingaling,' Jane-Mary said. 'You know you really pulled our chestnuts out of the fire.'

'Chestnuts?' Tingaling asked not understanding.

'Sorry, what we mean is you are a real brick.'

'Brick?' Tingaling queried again.

'What we are trying to say, is that you are wonderful.' Mary- Jane said, stopping herself just in time from saying, 'you saved our bacon.'

Tingaling beamed, just then Grant returned and had an urgent whispered conversation with Bruce. Bruce clapped his hand to his forehead. 'What are we to do? We go live in two hours and Gloria is plastered. Believe me, heads will roll and one of them will be yours.'

Suddenly all eyes turned to Tingaling who looked worried and could not think what she had done wrong. Busby, who had spent the last couple of hours laying the table in the dining hall with Victorian splendour, passed carrying a massive silver fruit bowl complete with tumbling grapes.

'Busby, would it be all right if we borrowed Tingaling for the shoot? Gloria is indisposed and we are at our wits end. She is a natural for television, and otherwise we will have to pack up and disappoint a lot of people.'

'If Lady Phyllis and Sir Jolyon, and of course Tingaling say yes, then that's fine with me.' Busby said, resting the heavy bowl down on the kitchen table, 'I think she will enjoy showing what a wonderful cook she is, better than most I have seen on television. Do you think you can do it Tingaling?'

'No problem,' Tingaling said smiling broadly, 'just write down the menu and I will get going with these two girls' help.'

Upstairs, Lady Phyllis rifled through the dresses hanging in her wardrobe.

'Too modern, not posh enough, too tight, must skip the puddings, ah, that will do if I put mother's fox fur round my shoulders. I will say Foxy is made of nylon if anyone asks.'

After a quick shower, Lady Phyllis fought her way into the purple satin number with heavy fringe in various strategic places, and then placed her favourite diamond tiara on her head. She liked the reflection that stared back at her in the long mirror. Dated enough to have been at a dinner party with Mrs Beeton, but underlining her position as Hostess.

Tripping down the corridor, she knocked on the door of the Jade guest bedroom where her cousin Gwen and her husband Rufus were getting ready.

'Come in.' Gwen said, in a Scottish accent.

Lady Phyllis liked to tell people that her cousin lived in a turreted crofter's hut in the Scottish Highlands. In fact, it was in one of the oldest castles in Scotland.

Gwen and Rufus were attired from head to foot in their family's tartan, even to the tartan socks on the knobbly, stocky legs of the red bearded Fergus.

'Well done you two', Lady Phyllis said, 'A splendid effort, give those television Johnnies something to focus on.'

In the kitchen, things hummed along with an efficient Tingaling consulting the Mrs Beeton's 'dinner for six persons' menu. 'They did eat a lot in those days,' she remarked with horror, 'I will cut it down a bit or Sir Jolyon will blow up.'

Juno took Tingaling away from her pots and pans and transformed her into a fairy princess with doe eyes and dark red lips. 'Is that really me?' she said, 'I love it, I look like a film star.'

'You are a star, darling.' Juno said, applying green eye shadow and jet black mascara to her already long eyelashes.

Lady Phyllis having been briefed on the fact that Gloria was sleeping it off in the Chinese bedroom upstairs, phoned Madge from her sitting room.

'Madge dear, 'she said when Madge answered, 'we have a situation here, Gloria is a lush and is in no fit state to do the show. It seems that Tingaling has been persuaded to take over. The powers-that-be want the finale to be six of us having a dinner party and polishing off the grub. Can you come and be a guest and bring Professor Wolfe along as well if possible?'

This was music to Madge's ears. Not only to hopefully meet Gloria, but to also appear on Television.

'Of course, I will contact William right away and then find something suitable to wear.'

'Thank you Madge, as old fashioned as you like. In about hours' time then, goodbye'

Later in the kitchen, the filming had started and was going out live. Tingaling had made the oyster patties and was making the curried rabbit. The partridges, wrapped in bacon were in the oven, the soup keeping warm on the hob and the steak bubbling in a thick sauce made with red wine. Mary-Jane and Jane-Mary were ready to plate up once the guests were seated.

Madge and Professor Wolfe made a dramatic entrance. Madge wearing the dress she had worn when playing the part of the governess in the Am Dram production of "The King and I" and the Professor in a swirling cape over his black tails and white wing collar,

81

with just a glimpse of a brocade waistcoat and gold watch chain.

They took their seats at the fabulously appointed table, and were introduced to Gwen and Rufus.

'Having a sleepover here on their way to see two of their horses run at Kempton Park races.' Sir Jolyon said by way of explanation. He was sitting at the head of the table in his ancient Saville Row dress suit that had been black, but after years of wear had now taken on a greenish tinge. Today, his feet were playing him up so he was still wearing his bedroom slippers, however, as they were under the table no one was any the wiser.

The red light on the camera glowed, meaning they were going out live as Busby entered with the trolley bearing a tureen of Vermicelli soup, and ladled it into soup bowls. He then served each diner carefully from the right. The conversation sparkled as the scene switched back and forth between the kitchen and the diners.

The partridges garnished with white grapes and served with game chips and bread sauce, were declared a triumph, as was the Steak, with its rich gravy and a variety of Julienne vegetables.

Each course was met with fulsome praise, especially the curried rabbit.

'Just how I had curry served when I was running the family tea plantation in Sri Lanka' Rufus said approvingly, 'Curry diagonally on one side of the dish and rice the other, separated by little pots made from sliced, empty red chillies with tiny heads of parsley in them. That was the life'

The Apple fritters, fresh orange Jelly and tartlets of greengage jam, were there if anyone had any room left, however, only token tasting took place.

Busby had filled their glasses up as they became empty and served a different wine with each course.

'No wonder they were enormously fat or died young if this was how people entertained in Mrs Beeton's day' Madge observed.

'And this is after cutting out several things from her menu, like fried slices of Cod and Anchovy sauce, John Dorey, Rissoles, Leg of Mutton and Plum pudding,' Lady Phyllis added.

A flushed, smiling Tingaling in her white Chef's uniform was in the final shot as the credits rolled. While the cameras were still on, Gloria lurched into the kitchen.

Framed in the doorway she yelled, 'Right I am ready Director, what is that Dragon Lady doing? Get rid of her, Grant, quick.'

'Too late Gloria, the Dragon Lady has just finished your programme and done a wonderful job of it.' Bruce said coldly

Madge appeared with her mobile phone. 'Can I have a selfie with you Gloria?' she asked.

'No, you can't, and everyone is fired,' Gloria shouted, exiting via the back door, followed by the faithful Grant.

Bruce called after her retreating figure. 'It's you that are fired Gloria.'

Turning to Tingaling he said, 'I would like to offer you the series, I will make you the biggest star on television, what do you say?'

Tingaling thought for a long minute then shook her head. 'I love being here with Lady Phyllis and Sir Jolyon, so thank you, but I do not want to leave Frogitt Hall. You can pay me for today, no problem.'

Next day the headlines were all about last night's fantastic cookery programme with an unknown star. Lady Phyllis was thrilled that Frogitt Hall was on the map and decided to capitalise on the publicity by opening it to the public.

'Tingaling, Sir Jolyon and I are pleased that you wish to stay with us. When we open the Hall to the public, if we turn one of the outbuildings into a restaurant, would you like to run it for us?'

Clapping her hands, Tingaling said excitedly, 'you bet, I will do a good job of it, you see, Gloria real bad person the girls say.' Her grasp of the English language was getting better every day.

Madge had set her television to record the programme, and sat for hours looking at herself on the screen. No one who called escaped a viewing.

The Passing of Howard

A sad event happened in Greater Humpton village, Howard Balcombe, one-half of the couple known mainly for their nudism, passed away. To every one's surprise, he turned out to have left instructions for a church service and burial in the local cemetery.

The choice of coffin was a woven wicker coffin, which was resting in the nave of the church, on a wooden stand with the lid off. A naked Howard lay with most of him luckily covered by wild flowers, picked from the Fen by a chanting group of nudists.

Joan had arranged for a Company to video the service and made sure that she was always in shot, registering every emotion from brave smiles to hysterical collapse as the organist swung into 'We Shall Overcome' at the end. Joan, luckily was clothed in a sort of High Priestess robe with a coronet of wild flowers.

'I thought Howard would have been all New Age and want something a bit more hippy than a proper service in a proper church.' Daisy Biggers said to her husband Bert as the mourners all trooped to the King's Arms public house after the service. Daisy and Bert had become quite friendly with the Balcombes after they went on a Mystery Weekend with them. The only mystery was why they had bothered to go in the first place; it had been a pathetic flop.

'I think Howard thought it was going to be one of those wife swapping dos.' Daisy confided to Miranda, when she enquired if they had enjoyed themselves.

'Poor Howard, he always thought that there was a wild party somewhere and he could never find it.' Miranda said, showing, for her an amazing insight into Howard's leanings.

In the pub, Madge sat next to Howard's sister, Patricia who had travelled from High Wycombe for the funeral. 'I am so sorry for your loss,' Madge said, 'how did it happen?'

Patricia sniffed in a disapproving way. 'Drafts you know, the cold variety! Well of course, if you run around with no clothes on and sit in a draft that is what happens. Howard always had a weak chest, so he caught a chill that turned into pneumonia. I blame Joan, always sleeping with the windows wide open, even in the middle of winter. Do you know he told me he used to wake up some days covered in snow as he was the one who slept nearest to the window?'

'Good Lord,' Madge exclaimed, 'my dogs sleep, winter and summer, by an electric fire. I keep two bars on for them. They are Chihuahuas and feel the cold, being from Mexico.'

'Patricia obviously had no time for her sister-in-law. 'Do you know before Howard met Joan he was a much-respected bank manager? However, once they got together it was all downhill.'

Madge tried to imagine Howard as a bank manager but it was beyond her. What she was dying to tell Patricia, but thought better of it, was that once she had to fight off the advances of an over keen Howard, which had come as a shock to her.

Patricia had another Sherry and warmed to her theme of it all being Joan's fault that her brother was lying in his grave. 'She rewrote the rules for musical chairs and made it musical men. That was before they moved to Greater Humpton. Howard joined a choir and she ran through them like a dose of salts.'

At that moment, Joan came up and sat in the seat next to Patricia. Grasping her hand, she said amid gulps and tears, 'You two are giving me such comfort, Madge always so strong and Patricia never short of a kind word of support. Did someone say you are going to the Greek Islands Madge? Howard and I spent many happy summers there.'

'Yes I am going with William Wolfe, you know the professor from Waddlington Major. We are going to recapture our lost youth, well that is our hope.' Madge said, pleased to see the surprise in Joan's eyes and knowing it would now be discussed all around the Pub. 'Never too old to expand one's horizons.'

Joan looked dreamy for a while. 'Do you know when we were in Corfu we hired one of those small 50cc motor bikes, the ones the travel agents tell you to avoid. Many holidaymakers fell off them, and the mark of shame was the purple disinfectant that medics applied. People sniggered when the unfortunate people with purple patches walked into their hotel's dining room.'

Howard and I hired one of those motor bikes and all was fine on the first day. The next day we rode on it up to the mountain area. At the top was a quarry and when we tried to go through the stony surface the bike came to a dead stop and we fell with the bike, still running on top of us. As we lay there a car with a German number, plate pulled up, there was no one else around. The driver walked over to us, looked down and said, 'Do you have the time?' Being typically English, Howard looked at his watch, 'It is a quarter past eleven,' he said from his prone position. The German driver turned on his heel and walked away leaving us still under the bike. We had scraped most of our tan off down one side of our bodies. However, we were not badly hurt. We got back on the bike and finished up at a beach; where we walked into the sea and washed off the blood and chalky dust. Funnily enough, we healed very quickly and did not need a purple daubing. It was one of the most bizarre happenings of our lives.

'How very unkind, too tight to buy a watch or was he just being Teutonic?' Madge said getting up from her seat, 'I must go and finish my packing, we are off to the airport tonight. So nice to have met you Patricia.' She kissed Joan. 'Bear up my dear, Howard would have been proud of your resilience today.'

'Charming lady,' Joan remarked, 'heart and soul of our village. Howard was a great admirer of Madge. Well I must mingle so many kind people to thank.'

Phoebe Perkins and her husband, Thomas immediately took the seats that Joan and Madge had just left. 'That was a lovely service; it is nice that Joan recorded it on video.' Phoebe said,

Patricia looked as if she would explode. 'I think that was so vain, no better than the way people record everything that is on a plate in front of them. What is wonderful about a sloppy curry eaten in some grubby café? We have had wonderful curries in India, now that is something to put on your Face Book page.'

Trying to lighten the mood, Thomas said 'is that your husband at the bar, the one recounting his many ' holes in one' at his Golf Club?'

Patricia smiled at last. 'Yes, that is Morris, he is the Captain this year; we have just had our Ladies' Night. We are very much looked up to at the Club. We are so pleased that Howard and Joan lived here and not in High Wycombe.

Just then, voices were raised in the knot of men round the bar and someone said,

'Oh, knock it off, go back to High Wycombe, we have no interest in your Golf Club or your Caribbean Cruises.'

'If I remember rightly', another voice chimed in, 'you were taken off the liner and flown home after you caught that gastro bug thing.'

Someone else joined in, 'Your parents could not even spell your name correctly, called you after a car, didn't they Morris?'

Morris was now very red in the face. 'Come on Patricia, let's go, now Howard has gone we will never have to come here ever again.'

Patricia and Morris left the pub and getting into their matching sports cars, they drove off to cheers and catcalls from the assembled crowd of mourners.

'That was a passing to remember, Just proves you can choose your friends but not your relatives.' Phoebe said to Drusilla Harris. They clinked glasses.

'A shame Howard missed today's event, mind you he was a randy old goat.' Drusilla winked at Phoebe who giggled and nodded in agreement.

'Oh dear,' Drusilla said, 'funerals are supposed to be very sober affairs, but I reckon Howard would have enjoyed his. Can't wait to see Joan's video.'

Phoebe nodded. 'That will be a classic, and the only one starring Joan that she can show the vicar'

Humpton's New MP

There was great excitement at the election of a new Member of Parliament for the Humpton Constituency. Bernard Danvers had stood as the Independent candidate after Helen Travers had resigned in a huff after losing her job as Rural Affairs Minister in the recent reshuffle. Helen had blotted her copybook by taking the affairs bit of her job description too literally, and going on too many overseas jollies with another married politician. There was nothing rural about these trips, and she had never been seen in wellies or near a living and breathing farm animal. The male politician's wife had sued for divorce, and Helen had been sent packing from her Ministerial job.

Bernard Danvers was a dish, and had managed to turn Helen's nine hundred majority into a thousand plus win while standing as an Independent. He was tall and slim and had a calm and well-mannered way of speaking that caused people to stop and listen. His wealthy parents had sent him to a very good school and he had left University with a degree in Classics and Law. Before throwing his hat in the ring to become Humpton's Member of Parliament, he had bought a converted windmill in Little Humpton and written several rather heavy books about ancient civilisations. Bernard still resided in the Humpton Windmill and listed cider making among his hobbies.

During the by-election, Bernard campaigned assiduously and called on every one of the voters to outline his policies. This went down well with the Humpton residents. If someone was up a ladder he would stop and chat to the person at the top, every farm and smallholding was visited, and the owners of village shops had a chance to air any grievances. The verdict was that Bernard was a good egg and his campaign featured on local and national television.

Fanny Jones was part of his band of helpers delivering leaflets and stuffing personal messages into envelopes. Bernard struggled at the computer and Fanny watching him said, 'Let me do that for you.'

Although Fanny was considered a duffer at most things and lacked confidence, she was an expert on a computer. 'It is just the way my brain is wired.' she would say, as her fingers flew over the keys.

Bernard observing this waited for a quiet moment when the others had left and asked if she would like to be his Personal Assistant, Researcher and general Girl Friday. Fanny went red and protested that she would be a disaster.

'No, you would be very good at it and I really need your help.' Bernard said, fixing Fanny with his rather short sighted, blue eyes from behind large horn rimmed glasses.

Put like that Fanny could not refuse. 'What name were you christened?' Bernard enquired, 'I don't believe it was Fanny.'

'Frances Joy.' A still blushing Fanny replied.

'Then from now on you are Frances, and we will discuss your salary once you have told your husband about my offer.'

Fanny paused and thought about the suggestion. 'Yes, Frances is much more the name of a Personal Assistant, I like that.' she smiled at Bernard who smiled back. He did have a lovely smile. It had been on the campaign posters but this was a soft smile that reached his blue eyes and she felt her pulse quicken.

When Fanny excitedly told Harold the next day at breakfast about the job offer, he scoffed in his usual sarcastic way.

'What you being a Personal Assistant? What is the man thinking about? You will not last a day.'

Fanny had endured these put-downs from the minute the ring was on her finger after their wedding. She had never fought back, but she really wanted this chance to do something that she knew she could make a success of.

'Well Harold I am going to take that job and you are not going to stop me. Also from now on I am going to call myself Frances which as you know is my proper name'

In the five years they had been married, Frances had meekly accepted all the sneering remarks that Harold had tossed her way, until she really believed she was useless. Now realising someone thought she was clever made all the difference.

With that, she slammed out of the house and drove to Greater Humpton, which possessed an upmarket fashion shop. After trying on several outfits, she bought a very smart navy blue suit and a three quarter length bright red coat. She enjoyed the assistant's flattering patter, and even if it was only sales talk, it made her feel happy.

'You have such a lovely slim figure and being quite tall you can wear the latest fashion trends.' The assistant said, putting the purchases into a big carrier bag with the name of the shop printed on it.

Next Frances went to Gary's Hair Salon. 'Can you fit me in for a cut and blow dry please Gary? I know it is short notice but I want a new look to go with my new clothes.'

'I have been dying to get my hands on your hair Fanny, professionally speaking. Now take a seat and tell me what you have in mind.'

Frances stared at herself in the mirror, 'I don't know Gary, just make me beautiful.'

Frances's long hair was a light brown and straight, she usually had it tied back with an elastic band. As Gary combed it out it proved to be thick and strong.

'Today I will just cut it in a shoulder length bob and next time we could try some blonde high lights. What do you say?'

Frances nodded happily. After the shampooing, she watched as Gary snipped away. As the hair fell to the floor, her spirits lifted. This is a new me, she thought. When Gary had finished, and showed her the back in the mirror Fanny laughed with delight.

'I look quite nice', she said modestly.

'Quite nice, you look knock out,' Gary said, 'now don't forget the highlights, so come and see me again soon.'

Frances paid and virtually danced out of the shop. On an impulse, she drove to the Mill hoping Bernard was not out. The Mill was on the edge of Little Humpton village,

Humpton River flowed past and in winter rushed past and under its rustic bridge. It was a very pretty scene and had featured on many postcards.

'Hello Frances, do come in,' Bernard said answering her knock on the stable type door. 'My goodness you do look pretty today'.

'Thank you, Bernard,' a blushing Frances said, 'I have come to say I would like to accept your offer of a job, can we discuss the details?'

Seated in Bernard's office he said, 'Did your husband like the idea of you working for a Politician?'

The old Fanny would have lied but the new Frances shook her head, 'What he likes and dislikes does not matter anymore, it is what I want that matters now.'

'Atta girl! I am glad you are going to take the job; we will make a good team. How did you meet Harold?'

'It was at a Summer school, he is an English teacher and had a class of overseas students, and I was doing a Computer course. We met in the college dining room, he is much older than I am. At first, he was charming and I was swept off my feet. However, once we were married he changed and now I am fed up with him always being critical. It would be fair to say I do not even like him now.'

Bernard shook his head. 'A sad state of affairs, I have never married, of course if the right girl came along, who knows.'

They discussed the salary, holiday entitlement and other details. 'You will be expected to come with me to the Houses of Parliament, I have an office there and also I am in the process of buying a small flat in London which will cut down the travelling.'

Frances grew more optimistic by the minute. Although she had liked the quiet backwater of Little Humpton, she was young and the thought of getting to be part of life in the Capital was exciting.

'Can you start next Monday? The recess is over and we have Prime Minister's Questions on Wednesday.'

It proved to be a real learning curve for them both. Getting to know how everything worked took a while but they were young and keen. The older members smiled when the two young people entered the tearoom as it reminded them of when they first started.

Several Editors sent journalists to interview Bernard and he appeared on 'Have I Got News for You' and held his own against the regular panellists. Yes, Bernard Danvers, MP had arrived.

In Little Humpton, an incident was causing much concern. An ancient caravan turned up in the village car park and obviously meant to stay. It came with two mangy dogs, a rusty car, a smoking open barbecue and several grubby children. Notices were served and ignored and the Police were called. Nearby residents came to see Bernard and asked him to see if he could find a way of resolving this situation. Bernard's Law background proved a help and eventually the unwelcome visitor was forced to move on.

The Constituency office where Bernard held his weekly Surgeries was in a converted barn attached to the Mill. Frances was sitting in her smaller office typing up some notes when she heard a commotion. She had just shown a scruffy man who gave his name as Mr Alf Smithers in to see Bernard. Grabbing a large paperweight, she opened the connecting door between the two offices and saw Mr Smithers wielding a knife at Bernard and shouting that he now had nowhere to put his caravan. She crept up and brought the marble paperweight down on Mr Smithers' balding head, and he crashed to the floor, the knife slithering away.

Bernard then called the Police and before the assailant regained consciousness, he was carted off to jail. Bernard and Frances drank several glasses of his excellent cider to calm their nerves and were quite relaxed when reporters and a TV crew arrived to interview them. They were instantly famous, and even Harold arrived and went on camera to say how brave his wife had been.

Next day's headlines not only carried the story of the incident at the Mill but also that of a Mrs Beryl Jones who claimed she was the wife of Harold Jones. They had not lived together for over ten years and Harold had not bothered to divorce her before tying the knot with Frances. This made Harold a bigamist, and Frances a single woman. Harold protested that he had completely forgotten about Beryl; however, the Police thought this was unlikely as Beryl was a very large lady and hard to forget.

When they were eventually alone in Bernard's office, he gazed across the desk where a shattered Frances sat.

'Darling, Frances' he said quietly in his lovely voice, 'now you are a single person do you think we can be a couple, an item, whatever they call it these days and see how we get on? As I said, I never wanted to be tied to anyone before, however, now it is different. Let me look after you. Perhaps if it works out we can make things permanent.'

The noise of the river sounded very loud as Frances considered this surprising offer. Eventually she tapped away on her computer.

Then a message came up on Bernard's IPad. It read, 'Dear Bernard, yes please X.'

Jackdaws' Heath Road

There was a road on the outskirts of Greater Humpton that had either a bad reputation or an interesting one, which varied according to your viewpoint. To those who read the more scandalous newspapers it was interesting, as various white-collar criminals bought houses there because it was very rural and the large houses lay well back from the road. For the upright citizens, it did lower the tone of the village. However, the owners of the houses kept very much to themselves, and only their large cars with smoky black windows occasionally drove through the village, and their children sometimes rode their ponies along the country lanes. Diamond Jake also had his property at the end of Jackdaws' Heath Road.

Betsy Rowe, who ran the local Post Office and the Yoga Evening class, had a daughter called Bella although her full name was Annabella. Betsy was always a bit vague about Bella's father who was never around. Bella had been the star pupil when she had attended Mrs Trudy Swan's dance school, called rather cutely, 'The Cygnets School of Drama and Dance.'

Bella was their leading light and went on to get every award possible, and so many certificates that Mrs Swan could hardly sign them quick enough, and Betsy ran out of walls to hang them on.

When Bella was eighteen, she joined a dance company that toured the world and eventually finished up several years later at a nightclub in The Balearics. In the

Post Office, customers, who had asked how Bella was getting on, were a bit flummoxed by the Balearics bit but nodded knowingly and went home to consult their atlas and find out where it could be.

'My Bella is working so hard that she has acquired a couple of apartments, several big cars, some wonderful diamond rings and other jewels.' A proud Betsy would say as she counted out stamps and weighed parcels. Only a few more worldly customers raised eyebrows as they counted their change.

One day an excited Betsy told her Yoga class that Bella and her boyfriend had put in an offer for Nuthatch House, a large property with a gatehouse in Jackdaws Heath Road, and that their offer had been accepted. Several weeks later, many vans arrived outside Nuthatch House. Expensive carpets were fitted, a new kitchen was installed and furniture from London's best emporiums trundled in through a newly installed electric gate.

Betsy was beside herself with joy. 'Just think my lovely Bella is right back here in the village, I will be able to catch up with all that has been going on since she left home.' she confided to a tanned Madge, who had returned from her travels in the Greek Islands with William.

'I am so glad for you,' Madge said, 'have you met the boyfriend yet?'

'Rodney took Bella and me for dinner at the Golden Cockerel Restaurant the other night, he is a bit older than Bella but charming.'

'The Golden Cockerel,' Madge mused, 'very expensive, what does Rodney do for a living?'

'Oh he is a Property Developer in the Balearics and has a boat building firm out there and a few financial businesses. He was telling me his hobby is making ceramic pots and he is building a kiln in the garden of Nuthatch House.'

'I am dying to meet him, he sounds a most interesting person.' Madge said, as she put a friendly hand on Betsy's arm. 'Must get on, so much to catch up with when you have been away.'

'What do you make of that, William?' Madge said later. After she and William had holidayed together, they felt they had each met their soulmate, but agreed to keep living in their own houses.

William smiled knowingly, 'Call me a cynic Madge, however, I think Betsy had better make the most of the situation while she can.'

A few months later, a newspaper ran a story of an irate woman who claimed that her husband, Rodney Smart had dumped her for a pole dancer called Bella Rowe. Mrs Smart added that Rodney had 'set Bella up in a house in Greater Humpton' and was flitting between his business empire, a Villa in Spain where she lived, and his young mistress.

There had been many complaints regarding Rodney Smart's business transactions over the years. The Police called at Nuthatch House and after a thorough search, nothing illegal was found. However, it transpired Rodney had a very colourful past. It was rumoured that when growing up in London Rodney had been linked to several large heists and that was the reason that he had set up his businesses abroad.

Betsy braved it out and turned up for work at the post office as usual. She was about to close up for the day, and was counting and itemising the money before locking it in the safe, when a masked man burst in through the door. There was no one else in the Post office as the last customer had just left.

'This is a hold up, put all that money in a bag or you get it.' The gruff male voice said from behind a ski mask as he waved an evil looking gun. A startled Betsy was about to do as she was told then paused; there was something familiar about the voice.

'Wally, is that you? Is this what you have come down to after all these years?'

The robber lowered his gun. 'Betsy, I didn't know it was you, I am really sorry to frighten you. How have you been?'

'So much for your concern Wally, we have a daughter who is the girlfriend of Rodney Smart, he will not take kindly to this.'

'Rodney 'the grudge' Smart?' That is big league Betsy. This gun isn't real and I've fallen on really hard times, or I would not have done this job. Can we forget about it?'

With that, Wally put the gun in his pocket and took off the ski mask.

Betsy thought for a second, then said, 'Ok Wally, for our daughter's sake I will. Come and see me soon and promise me you will go straight, or I will tell Rodney.'

The shop door opened and PC Fred Constable looked in as he did his final security round of the day.

'Everything all right Betsy?' he said.

'Fine thank you Fred, the last customer is just leaving.' Fred stood aside as Wally walked past him.

'Goodnight Betsy.' The policeman said as he shut the door.

A week or so later Wally was introduced to his long-lost daughter, or to be more precise it was the father who had been lost not his daughter. They got on like a house on fire and Rodney also took to Wally.

'Dad come and live here in our Gatehouse,' Bella said, 'and when Rodney and I are out of the country you can look after the place until we come back.'

This solved Wally's housing crisis. He also made a hit with their two big mastiff dogs, which was lucky as they roamed around the grounds for security and were not the type you patted or threw sticks for them to retrieve.

There was a police raid on Diamond Jake's property next door. Sirens wailed and Jake was escorted to the waiting police van. Two junior officers were posted outside the gates while the search went on inside.

Rodney casually strolled up to them. 'So glad you are cleaning up the area.' he said, his eyes twinkling behind his dark glasses. 'People like him lower the tone of the neighbourhood. By the way, me and Bella are off in the Helicopter to Spain today, cheers boys.'

As he strolled back to the house one of the policemen said, 'Slippery one that, always a move in front of us, we will get the blighter one day.' Ten minutes later Rodney's helicopter with him at the controls and Bella as passenger, left for sunnier climes.

Mystical Happenings

Lady Francesca arrived at Frogitt Hall a day earlier than expected. She had driven from her extensive Tudor estate with her son, Duke, short for Marmaduke.

'Couldn't stand another minute with Sebastian and his shooting and fishing friends.' Francesca said by way of explanation, as she swept inside and waved an imperious hand at her Rolls parked outside. 'Get your man to park the beast and get our luggage up to our rooms.'

'Hello Francesca, I see the years have not mellowed you.' Sir Jolyon remarked with a laugh. He was fond of his cousin's second wife, who had grown up in Hungary and considered herself above any of Sebastian's relatives.

'Sorry darlink,' Francesca said, she had never lost her Hungarian accent. 'The roads were full of other people and it causes me pain.' Francesca always thought she should have outriders clearing a path for her when she drove anywhere. Although Sebastian had a chauffeur, he refused to drive Francesca, and threatened to resign when asked.

Lady Phyllis strode in through the French doors from the garden where she had been relaying her instructions for the following day to the outside staff.

'My word Francesca, you are early, a day early in fact. I like punctuality but this is carrying it a bit far.'

Sensing the tension Duke stepped forward and smiled. 'Hello, it is lovely to see you both again.' Duke had inherited his father's charm and not his mother's forceful nature.

'Goodness me Duke, you have grown up so much since you were last here. How old are you now?'

'He is eighteen and going to University in September where he will definitely beat all the other students, you'll see.' His mother said proudly, while Duke blushed and looked embarrassed.

Busby had seen the car arrive and soon all was in order. Car parked, luggage upstairs and Francesca and Duke seated ready for lunch. Tingaling, never one to be caught short in the food stakes had soup, cold salmon in aspic, new potatoes, mixed green salad and apple pie with custard ready for Busby to serve.

'What a gem you have there, where did you find her?' Francesca said as she cleared her plate and nodded to Busby for seconds.

'Now Francesca, you try and steal her and we are going to fall out.' Lady Phyllis said firmly, 'Tingaling has already turned down the offer of a big television programme to stay with us. So you have been warned.'

After lunch, Duke sat with his mobile phone, his fingers a blur. His mother sighed. 'Never without that wretched phone, what do they find to put on those chat things?'

To change the subject Lady Phyllis said, 'Are you still doing your séances?'

'Of course,' Francesca replied, 'but only for our charity days. People tell me I am very talented and that my predictions come true. I have a sixth sense about people and places. I feel you have an undiscovered secret somewhere here in Frogitt Hall.'

At that moment, Tingaling came in with a tray of tea.

Francesca's hand flew to her chest. 'My God, what a lovely person,' she gasped raising her eyes to the ceiling. 'I have just had a message from my Guide, she says this lovely girl was an Eastern Princess many years ago in ancient times.'

'And I am Henry the Eighth.' Sir Jolyon muttered under his breath.

Tingaling nearly dropped the tray. 'That will be all thank you Tingaling.' Lady Phyllis said to a wide-eyed Tingaling after she had put the tray on the low occasional table.

'Me a Princess?' Tingaling's smile could not have been wider. 'I will go and tell Busby, he very lucky man.'

'Adorable,' breathed Francesca, 'we must get out your Ouija board tonight Phyllis and see what it can tell us.'

Phyllis stopped with the teapot poised in her hand and said, 'All right Francesca but don't fill Tingaling's head with a lot of twaddle, she is very impressionable, keep telling her she was a Princess and we will never hear the last of it.'

'But Malinka, my Spirit Guide just sent me that message so it must be true. We will ask her tonight.'

Later that afternoon Sir Jolyon looked out of the window and saw Francesca walking slowly round the lawn with a forked willow branch held out in front of her.

'What is your mother up to now?' he said to Duke, who was sitting tapping out messages on his mobile phone.

'I think she is trying to locate buried treasure, she is convinced there is some hidden here.'

Sir Jolyon nodded his head. 'Yes there have always been rumours. Many have tried to find it and all have failed. I feel your mother will be disappointed.'

Duke smiled and went back to his messages.

An excited Francesca later reported that the divining rod had dipped several times as she walked round the garden. Lady Phyllis was not impressed. 'Of course it did,' she said witheringly, 'it was indicating there was water beneath the ground. We know there are underground springs here however, that is not treasure.'

Francesca gave her a pitying smile. 'You will eat your words darlink, you just wait.' she said and went upstairs to change into an impressive beaded black dress and a tiara slightly bigger than the one worn by Lady Phyllis.

After dinner when it was dark outside and the curtains were drawn, the Ouija board was fetched and placed on the smaller table in the morning room. Tingaling joined the others who were sitting round it with an upturned glass in the middle of the board. The only light came from several flickering candles that threw ghostly shadows on to the walls hung with portraits of long departed ancestors.

'Now first we must hold hands and really believe that we can summon up my Guide who is called Malinka',

Francesca said solemnly. 'Now say after me, Spirit of the past move among us.'

They all did dutifully say the words as instructed, nothing happened.

'Now come along Malinka we are waiting, just give us a sign. Everyone let us repeat our opening chant but with a bit more feeling, are we ready?'

'Spirit of the past move among us.' This time everyone said it much louder and there was a faint muffled sound.

'There you are Malinka, I hope you are feeling well.' Francesca was in her element. 'Now if we can all release hands and put a finger on the glass.' she commanded. 'I will ask the questions.'

When they had done this, she nodded and said, 'Was this lovely lady on my right ever ancient royalty?' The glass moved but did not touch any of the letters on the board.

'I will repeat my question Malinka, was this lady ever royalty?' The glass started to move, slowly at first then rapidly. It spelt out, yes.

'What was her rank?' The glass moved and spelt out, Princess.

Tingaling nearly spoke but Francesca gave a low shush.

'Is there any hidden treasure in this place?'

The glass was moving rapidly now, First to Y then E then S.

'Where, Malinka, where?' However, nothing happened. 'She is tired, we will try again tomorrow.'

Francesca said as Sir Jolyon blew out the candles and switched on the electric lights.

'I am a Princess.' Tingaling said grandly.

'A Princess we rely on for a drink.' Sir Jolyon said firmly. 'Can you please ask Busby to mix us all one of his wonderful gin and tonics and you can join us.'

'Thank you, but I would rather have a nice cup of green tea in the kitchen with Busby.' Tingaling smiled at them all and left the room.

'Sweet girl she really thinks the world of Busby.' Lady Phyllis said, and was going to explain about how Tingaling had been a mail order bride, but Duke, who was staring transfixed at his mobile phone, interrupted her.

'I have a message that has just come up on the screen. It is written in an old medieval script and reads, 'box in far wall of cellar, ten in, five up, Malinka.'

They all went cold. Francesca grabbed the phone. 'I hope you are not playing games Duke.'

'Mother I am as amazed as you are; it is not a type of script that I have ever seen before.'

Busby entered with a tray of drinks. 'Your gin and tonics as requested, Sir Jolyon.' He said putting the tray down on the table.

'Thank you Busby. It now transpires that you are married to a Princess, how do you feel about that?'

'Exactly the same as I did before.' Busby was not easily impressed and did not believe in spirits. He also did not wish to confess that the sound that they had heard when calling up the spirit had been him dropping a brush on the kitchen floor.

'Right,' Sir Jolyon said as he took a sip of his G&T, 'after we have had our drink, you and I Duke, will investigate the cellar, however, I do not expect it to reveal anything.'

Holding a large torch Sir Jolyon and Duke went down the cellar steps while Lady Phyllis and Francesca stood at the top craning their necks to try to follow the beam of the torch. The cellar walls were made of roughhewn blocks of stone.

'Ten in and five up, that must mean the blocks of stone but from which side, left or right?' Duke said, 'shall we try from the right side first?' He counted ten blocks along and then five blocks up. The torch held by Sir Jolyon shone on the stone as Duke tried to lever it out. It would not budge.

'Let's try from the left' Sir Jolyon said shining the torch on the other side of the wall and once again, they counted ten blocks in and five blocks up. The stone it lit appeared much looser, and Duke managed to get his fingers round it and after several tugs, it fell out. Inside was a wooden box. 'Hooray' yelled Duke, while Sir Jolyon said, 'Well I'll be a monkey's uncle!'

'What's going on down there?' Francesca shouted as she and Lady Phyllis got their tiaras locked trying to peer down the stairs.

After bringing up the box, which was covered in dust, they carried it into the kitchen. Busby and Tingaling crowded round. 'Open it Jolyon, I am shaking all over.' commanded Francesca who had righted her tiara while Lady Phyllis was too excited to worry about such details.

As Sir Jolyon lifted the lid, they all gasped. Inside was an array of sparkling jewels. Necklaces, rings, bracelets and brooches, all set with precious stones.

'Wow, get a load of that.' said Duke, 'they must be worth millions.'

'Obviously when these jewels were hidden it was the time of raids by various warring factions and if you were on the wrong side they took all your valuables. My ancestors hid their most precious belongings and obviously were not able to retrieve them.' Sir Jolyon said sadly. 'How amazing that for all our scepticism, your hunch was right Francesca. We must congratulate your Spirit Guide.'

Duke's phone bleeped. After reading the message, for the second time that night he said 'Wow!'

'What does it say?' an impatient Francesca demanded.

'The message reads 'Thank you, Malinka.' Duke announced to the dumfounded group.

'More gin and tonics?' queried Busby.

The Best Village Competition

On that wonderful night when the jewels were found Sir Jolyon looked round at the excited faces and said, 'We all played a part in this, so girls pick an item, Phyllis you first.'

Without hesitation, Lady Phyllis picked up a diamond necklace. 'I love this it matches my tiara. It needs a good clean and one day I will pass it on to our granddaughter.'

Next, it was Francesca's turn. She examined several pieces but settled for a ring with a single large diamond that reflected a fiery brilliance as it caught the light. 'Thank you, this will be the talking point back home and prove my occult talent.' Francesca had no time for modesty.

'Now Tingaling, you choose an item to enhance your Princess status.' Sir Jolyon smiled as he swept his hand over the remaining jewels spread out on the kitchen table. There was a long pause as Tingaling thought. Then she picked up a damaged brooch. The setting had all but fallen apart but it had two wonderful big diamonds and several smaller ones making up a leaf design.

'I would like this please and use the two big diamonds to make earrings. The smaller ones will pay for the cost of making them. When I am working I can always wear earrings anything else I would have to take off'

'Good thinking' Francesca said, 'you are a very bright girl.'

Among the rings that were obviously for ladies, there were a couple of heavy solid gold signet rings, one had M on it. Sir Jolyon handed it to Duke.

'Please take this ring as a reminder of your stay here at Frogitt Hall. It was your modern contraption that led us to the discovery.'

'What about you Jolyon?' Francesca said while admiring her ring that fitted perfectly.

'I will get the rest cleaned and valued. I may keep a few pieces but my pressing need is for capital. I am getting on and I have long needed an Estate Manager to look after the Hall and grounds, not to mention the attached farms and cottages. Then Lady Phyllis and I can visit our eldest son and heir who owns a big sheep farm in New Zealand. I hear that there may be a wedding soon between our granddaughter and a lovely English boy called Robert. He did a stint on their farm in his gap year and they are madly in love. Then we can go and stay with Sam, our youngest son who is living in Australia and see that exciting country. Phyllis has been nagging me for ages to go and see them. She still thinks they are twelve'

'Don't forget completing the conversion of the big barn into the restaurant for Tingaling to run, it is nearly complete but still needs some expensive equipment.' Lady Phyllis reminded him, ignoring the jibes, as she knew Sir Jolyon missed their sons as much as she did.

'Yes, we are nearly there, just a few more weeks to opening. You must come to that Francesca.'

'You bet darlink.' Francesca replied, stifling a yawn.

'Right I will put the rest of the jewels in the safe then it is off to bed. Goodnight everyone.'

With that, they all made their way upstairs. Busby went round, locked up and turned off the lights. 'Whatever next?' he said to himself.

After Sir Jolyon had raised a big sum of money from the sale of the spare jewels, an Estate Manager, called Maxwell Chandler took over the running of everything. Luckily, he was young and efficient so Sir Jolyon could relax and plan his antipodean trip.

Tingaling was interviewed on television about the forthcoming opening of the restaurant, 'Nothing too fancy' she said, when asked what would be on offer. 'Light snacks; perhaps a couple of hot dishes like meat pies or a curry and rice and of course a vegetarian dish and salad, plus homemade cakes.'

'That sounds great, I hear you are descended from an ancient, eastern noble line, what is your title?'

Quick as a flash she replied, 'Princess Ting Patna.' as at that moment she had been thinking about the rice with the curry.

'Hasn't that a more Indian influence than from an East Asian part of the world?' Craig the programme presenter asked with a puzzled look.

'My family moved around a lot.' Tingaling replied. She was actually beginning to believe all this, especially as she was wearing her sparkling diamond earrings, which shone like beacons from her ears.

Meanwhile, other things were on the calendar. Every year both Humptons entered the Best Village Competition and although they had been runners up for several years, they had never won the top spot. Keith Fowler had always been the mover and shaker in charge of Little Humpton's entry into the competition, however, this year he pleaded excessive calls on his time with being Mayor and asked Madge to take over.

'Darling I would have loved to do it but William and I have bought a camper van and are off soon to explore all the places in the British Isles that we have never visited.' William and Madge were like a couple of late developing teenagers and even the very correct William wore jeans, trainers and casual shirts when they drove off on their trips.

Jimmy Griggs was in his garden clearing up the last of the sad mess caused by the winter storms and heavy rainfall. Now that the first snowdrops were nodding in the breeze, gardeners were out in force and Jimmy, who hated mess, was out restoring order to his quite large patch.

Keith Fowler knocked on Jimmy's front door and not getting an answer went round to the back garden. Jimmy looked up from his raking of dead leaves as he heard Keith open the gate.

'Hi Keith, what brings you here, are you going to offer to help?'

'Quite the contrary, I was going to ask for your help.' Keith replied, 'I need someone to run the Best Village Competition, will you take it on please Jimmy?'

Jimmy felt rather pleased about this; He was an ex-army Brigadier and quite missed telling people what to do. 'Anything to help the village Keith. Let's go inside and you can fill me in with the details of what it entails over a coffee.'

Later when Keith had left, Jimmy drew up action plans and pinned them up on the notice board he kept in his kitchen. Several phone calls later, he had a working committee of local worthies, consisting of Bert and Daisy Biggers, Drusilla Harris, Pixie Dean and Joe Pickering. His final call was to Bernard Danvers their M P, who promised that if they won he would take the whole committee on a visit to Parliament and treat them to tea on the terrace.

Then Jimmy set to work calling on the people who definitely needed to smarten up their properties. Top of the list was Miss Millet who lived in Ivy Lodge. The front garden was on the main road into the village and was so overgrown it gave a bad image of the village from the start. Miss Millet had at one time been an avid gardener but now she was over ninety and never left the house, not even into her own garden. Armed with a large slab of gingerbread, Jimmy knocked on the front door of Ivy Lodge.

'Go away.' A quavery voice said. Jimmy knocked again.

'Didn't I say go away?'

'Can I come in and have a word with you.' Jimmy shouted through the letterbox, 'I am Jimmy Griggs from up the road and I have some gingerbread for you.'

The sound of bolts being drawn back went on for several minutes and a claw like hand came out of the gloom inside.

Jimmy held on to his bag of gingerbread. 'Can I talk to you first, please Miss Millet?'

Eventually the door opened wide enough for Jimmy to squeeze inside, then Miss Emily Millet turned and said, 'Follow me.' She hobbled down a dark hallway into an equally dark kitchen.

Jimmy looked round at the ancient old range with a metal teapot steaming on the top. The words of Bertha, the home help who had told him that all Miss Millet lived on was gingerbread and stewed tea rang in his head. Whatever you do refuse the tea, it has been stewing away for days and will rot your inside if you drink it, Bertha had warned.

Handing over his paper bag, Jimmy trying to be diplomatic in his refusal of tea said, 'No thank you I only drink coffee.'

Miss Emily Millet waved a dismissive hand. 'Coffee, horrible stuff, I used to go out with a Yank, who only drank coffee that was in the war' she sat down and gave a short laugh, 'Hank the Yank I called him, we used to jitterbug.'

Jimmy stared at Emily and tried to imagine her jitterbugging, it was not possible until he saw a picture of a young and pretty girl in a frame on the wall. 'Is that picture of you?' He asked.

'Emily nodded, 'That was when I was in the ATS,' she said smiling as she reminisced. Now Jimmy got the picture.

Remembering why he had come he said, 'Little Humpton is entering the Best Village Competition and I realise it is hard for you to have a nice tidy front garden, however, we have some volunteers who can come and tidy it for you. Is that all right?'

'They will steal things.' Emily did not trust anyone.

'No they are good people and I will come with them. You trust me don't you? I was a Brigadier in the Army, a professional soldier.'

Emily thought for a while. 'A soldier like me? Yes they may come but you must come with them and bring me gingerbread.'

Jimmy laughed and turned to leave. 'Good that's the deal then. I will let myself out and see you next week.'

Back home in his kitchen or operations room as he was beginning to think of it Jimmy drew up lists. The Green Spaces team, the Community Buildings team and the Resident's Gardens team. He entered Miss Emily Millet's name on the latter. Then stood back with satisfaction, getting the first entry was always the hardest part and then you were on your way.

Hearing that Greater Humpton was also getting organised, Jimmy set up a meeting in the Village Hall, leaflets were distributed and on the night, there was a good turnout. Jimmy and his committee sat up on the stage and he explained his plans. First, he outlined the tasks of the three teams and described what was involved.

The judging panel will start coming round in June or July and these visits continue throughout the summer. The name of the winning village will be announced in September, followed by a presentation in November. Jimmy then asked for volunteers who wanted to help, and quite a few hands shot up. Each person stood up and said what their contribution would be and he noted it down under the three headings.

'This is a very good start.' Jimmy said smiling round. 'If you are a volunteer, before you go out will you leave your name and contact number with members of the committee sitting up here on the platform, and you can always contact me at headquarters err.. I mean my home at any time. We will meet here in two weeks' time and I will have a list of places that need special attention. Now, the watch-words are smart and tidy, so let us put Little Humpton on the map.' There was a ripple of applause as people either made their way up to the table where the committee sat, or filed out.

Jimmy was in his element. His kitchen was a sea of yellow post-it notes and lists while he constantly referred to the weekly planner on his IPad.

The Green Spaces team, headed by Bert and Daisy Biggers, concentrated on places which included the grass verges, hedgerows, riverbanks, and the removal of litter. Joe Pickering and Drusilla Harris were in charge of Community Buildings. These were wide ranging, taking in the War Memorial, village sign and the ancient horse trough on the Green. Much hard work and modern sprays, cleaned and polished them until they shone.

Pixie Dean and some burly Scouts, and members of the body building team from the Gym made short work of tidying the less than pristine front gardens. Even Billy Pickering was on the team, but really so that his mother Pixie could keep an eye on him.

As June approached, Jimmy spotted a problem that was spasmodic therefore hard to solve. On Saturdays, the Pony Club rode out. There were three ponies each with an adorable moppet on board and they trotted round the country lanes and through Little Humpton. Dawn Keeble was in charge and was a stunning sight in her riding hat and jodhpurs. She was not to blame for the steaming deposits the ponies left however, it did not look good on the road if the judges came.

Jimmy had a word with Dawn who agreed to change her route and make for Greater Humpton. 'Jimmy even if we change our ride we still have to go through the village first.' the delightful Dawn said, gazing up at Jimmy from under the brim of her hat.

'No problem, I will station some troops with buckets and shovels on the route, just in case.'

'Of course Mr Griggs, I do so hope we win.' Dawn said, as she mounted her horse and trotted off with her little charges.

Lovely girl, Jimmy thought as he stared after her. I just wish I were ten years younger.

There was a small hiccup at the end of May when an open top lorry drove through Little Humpton at night and left plastic litter everywhere even strips of it hanging from trees. Jimmy suspected foul play by The Greater Humpton bunch. He quickly organised a litter patrol. The sight of grown men swinging from trees to remove the plastic, cheered on by villagers, was exciting and they soon had everywhere tidy again.

Standing on an upturned crate Jimmy said, 'Great community spirit in solving this crisis, thank you.' rather in the manner of a Field Marshal addressing his troops in the war.

The Judges, armed with clipboards, came round several times in June and at the beginning of July. A meeting to take place in September at Waddlington Major Village Hall was announced, and on that day, members of the committees of all the competing entrants took their seats.

There was an expectant hush as the head judge stood up and started a ten-minute talk, explaining how they marked entrants.

'Get on with it.' muttered Jimmy under his breath.

Then came a list of runners up and special mentions. Little Humpton was not among them.

'Finally, we come to the winning Village,' there was a dramatic pause and you could have heard a pin drop. 'The winner is Little Humpton Village.'

'Yes.' Shouted Jimmy, leaping out of his seat and shaking the hands of all the committee. 'I knew we could do it, well done everyone.'

'A worthy winner' said the Chairman 'We will see you at the presentation in November.'

Through gritted teeth Thomas Perkins, who was in charge of Greater Humptons entry offered his congratulations.

Grinning widely Jimmy shook his hand. 'If you need any spare plastic let me know.' He said, as Thomas looked sheepish.

In November most of Little Humpton piled into The Village Hall for the presentation. Sir Jolyon and Lady Phyllis sent their congratulations, and said they were sorry not to be there but they were having a wonderful time in New Zealand.

Madge and William interrupted their travelling to return tanned and happy while the tireless Tingaling and Busby provided refreshments.

'Congratulations and well done Little Humpton.' The head of the judging panel said, handing Jimmy the silver cup'

Jimmy graciously acknowledged it and thanked his team. 'Everyone has worked so hard for this. The whole Village has taken part with a wonderful community spirit.' he said, lifting the cup aloft to cheers.

From her seat in the audience, the divine Dawn smiled proudly. She and Jimmy had got to know each other quite well over the summer as Jimmy had watched her, and the pony club's progression through the village with his bucket and spade at the ready.

'I have always liked older men of the military type.' she confided to Madge as they munched on Tingaling's wonderful sausage rolls.

A week later a minibus left Little Humpton and arrived in London, then made its way to Westminster and the Houses of Parliament. Bernard Danvers MP was as good as his word. He and Frances Jones, his fiancée and PA, ushered the impressed members of the winning village committee on the promised tour. It was Prime Minister's Questions, so they watched from the Gallery.

Luckily, it was a warm and sunny autumn day so they had Tea on the terrace, which overlooks the wonderful sights of London and the River Thames.

'Thank you, Bernard, this has been an unforgettable experience. Three Cheers for our Member of Parliament, Little Humpton Village, and Great Britain.' Jimmy said, and they all cheered.

THE END